Hick Lawyer

By Corey Burns

For Nancy, Butch & Dennie

And my wife and daughters

Water's like me. It's laaazy….. Boy, it always looks for the easiest way to do things.
Bob Ross

Unhappy, Unhappy. You have no complaint. You are what you are and you ain't what you ain't. So listen up buster and listen up good. Stop wishing for bad luck and knocking on wood.

Dear Abby, by John Prine

1

For all his twenty-seven years on the bench, Judge Daniel Ostergart had spoken to every criminal defendant who came before him with calm and respect. But Jeremy Wilson was wearing the judge thin. Jeremy was in his mid-twenties, with the best years of his life already in his rearview mirror and fading fast. Jeremy had been a high school football hero, enjoying everything that came with that status in a small town. Teachers found reasons to give him extra-credit when grades were getting too low for him to play; cops tended to look the other way when it came to speeding, or alcohol possession. And, he had laid every girl in his class who would put out; and at least one student teacher. Then, Jeremy went to a small state college on a football scholarship, partied, blew out a knee, partied some more and flunked out at the end of his first year. He came home, took a construction job, kept on partying, and a year later, caught his first meth charge. A year after that came the burglary charge and a long term of probation that he had now violated for the third time.

Judge Ostergart spoke to Jeremy in a paternalistic tone. "You showed great promise once Mr. Wilson. You were looked up to in high school. Your parents love you very much and have always supported you." The Judge stopped to look over his glasses, around the empty gallery of the courtroom and then down at Jeremy. "Today is the first time I can recall that they have not been to court with you. But, I know that your father has been sick lately. I hope he is doing better." The judge paused now and raised his eyebrows. "I hope that you will do better, Mr. Wilson."

The Judge let out a thoughtful sigh before continuing. "I am going to put you back on probation one last time and that probation will run for two more years. I want you to make a fresh start of things Mr. Wilson." Jeremy stared down at the table in front of him with his hands in his pockets and nodded his head at everything the Judge had to say, as though he were actually listening.

"You've been pretty good in the past about paying your restitution. You don't have much left. I want you to get that paid off in the next twelve months."

The Judge paused again, looking over his glasses at Jeremy, trying to make an impression. "This truly is your last chance Mr. Wilson. The County Attorney, Mr. Pedersen, wanted me to send you to the penitentiary today. Don't make me regret not doing that."

Jeremy just kept nodding. He was still a good-looking kid, but he had a hardness to his looks that came later in life for most folks. His clothes were presentable, but old. The cuffs of his khakis were frayed, and they puddled a little over scuffed tennis shoes. The faded polo shirt, starting to wear around the collar, was tucked into an unbelted waistline that was accentuated by the early bloom of a gut that looked out of place on his otherwise lean body.

Jeremy's court appointed lawyer, Dexter Smith, hunched over the defense table furiously scribbling the terms of the probation the judge was reciting. In contrast to his client, Dexter was not lean. He was approaching middle-age. He was above average in height, and pudgy. He wore a cheap hopsack blazer of polyester blend and every time he bent down, the tail of the coat rose up enough to reveal that the khakis he wore were Dickies work pants. Dexter glanced over at Wilbur Pedersen quickly a time or two, seeing that the County Attorney was furious that Jeremy Wilson was not going to prison. Dexter knew how to get under Wilbur's skin. He did that sometimes, just for fun. He also knew when to avoid getting under Wilbur's skin, and this was one of those times, so he avoided eye contact with Wilbur.

Jeremy had done well his first couple of years on probation. Then the violations started, each a little worse than the last. And every time, Dexter got re-appointed to Jeremy's case. This last time, Dexter got the bond reduced so Jeremy could get out and get an updated chemical abuse evaluation. The evaluation had recommended inpatient treatment, which Jeremy walked out of after three days. So, he went home, went back to roofing and saw his local counselor twice a week, waiting to get sentenced. The last update from his counselor before sentencing showed progress to be "slow but positive; active state of change; motivation is external." That meant that Jeremy knew he had a problem and was working on it, but only hard enough to stay out of prison. It was just enough.

Dexter felt bad for Jeremy. Dexter knew that Jeremy wanted a different life. He also knew that Jeremy was slowly killing himself. Jeremy had confided in Dexter once "The girls I grew up with all wanted me, and the guys all wanted to be me. Now I'm just the guy putting the roofs on their houses."

When the judge finished, Dexter left the courtroom trying to avoid Wilbur. He reminded Jeremy to go directly to the probation office and tell them what the judge had just done. Then, Dexter walked the half block to his office, threw Jeremy's file on the desk, and went upstairs to his apartment to pack for a two-week vacation.

Jeremy walked down the hall, right past the probation office without even looking in that direction, and out the front door of the courthouse. He proceeded down the sidewalk four blocks until he came to the home of a friend he had been staying with. He grabbed a beer from the fridge, plopped down on the couch, pulled a joint from an old cigar box on the coffee table and began to celebrate his victory in court.

****

Dexter Smith walked back into his building about 9:00 p.m. two weeks later. He had spent his vacation crisscrossing the South East, visiting family and college friends scattered all over. He was tired and glad to be home.

To his right was the glass door of his law office. Ahead of him, the stairs that led up to his apartment. As he headed up the stairs, Dexter could hear the late dinner crowd through the wall on his left at Lee Ho Fook's. Dexter ate most of his meals there, and the owner just took the cost of those meals off the rent check he paid Dexter each month. When combined with his county contract for part-time public defender and juvenile court work, the rent from the restaurant was still more than Dexter needed to sustain himself. His office, his apartment and the Chinese restaurant made up most of his world and they were all neatly contained in the building he had somehow lucked into when real estate was crashing. The last major component to his life was The Pawnee Club, a couple of blocks down, where he drank, socialized as much as he was apt to do, and where most of his private cases came from; mostly simple divorces, but an occasional will needed to be drafted. Dexter had also met someone to go home with a time or two, but that had not happened in quite a while. Relationships had frustrated Dexter through-out his life, but that was becoming less of a problem for him the older he got.

Dexter pushed his way into the large loft apartment which consisted mostly of an open space that included the kitchen area, complete with washer and dyer, and a living area centered around his couch. There were two small rooms to the back, a bedroom where Dexter kept his clothes but rarely slept, because he slept mostly on his couch, and a large

4

bathroom with an old claw-footed tub that had no shower, but a hose with a shower head that ran from the faucet. The whole place was spartan.

Dexter took his suitcase into the kitchen and dumped the contents on the floor in front of the washer. Then he went into the bathroom, peed, washed his hands and face and lit a cigarette. He went to the couch, plopped down, checked the alarm clock, and set it. He debated whether to go down stairs to the restaurant for a bite but fell asleep before he could decide.

Dexter hit the snooze bar three times before finally getting up at 8:15 the next morning. He rolled off the couch and went to the kitchen to start coffee. He went to the bathroom where he peed, washed his hands and face and lit a cigarette. He knew he would have to shower and shave but didn't know how soon. He knew he didn't have any appointments scheduled. He was his own secretary and would never set appointments on his first day back from vacation. He would just have to check his phone messages and email down in the office to see if he had been appointed to any cases that would require his attention that day.

By 9:00 a.m. Dexter had had enough coffee and nicotine to start his day and was dressed enough to go downstairs to the office. He opened the office door to find a small pile of mail on the floor below the slot. Glancing through the mail, he saw nothing of urgency and threw it in the center of his desk. Next, he checked his phone messages and emails. There was only one thing of note there. Dexter had been appointed to represent one Donald Alan Birch in a criminal matter and Mr. Birch's preliminary hearing was set for that afternoon at 3:30.

A preliminary hearing meant a felony case. And unless it was a drug possession case or a straight forward burglary, a felony could mean serious work. Clients took their felony cases seriously, so did the prosecutors, and the cops, and the courts. If it was a very serious matter, Dexter may have to put in extra time on the case which would mean billing for hours over his regular contract time.

It was probably a drug case or a simple property crime. That was the kind of stuff Dexter usually got. There were two other lawyers in town with contracts like Dexter's to do public defender work. Tom McWilliams and John Miller were both from the area and had both been practicing law much longer than Dexter. Those two got the tough felony cases, not Dexter, unless there was some kind of conflict that prevented the other two from representing someone. Sometimes there were multiple defendants in a case. Each codefendant would get a different attorney, and if Dexter were one of those, he would just ride the coat tails of the other attorneys in the case. Dexter had no reason to think this new case would be anything but one of the simpler felony cases.

It wasn't so much that Dexter was lazy; which is what most people thought; he just lacked confidence. He never found anything he was particularly good at in high school. It took him a couple of years longer to finish college than most. When he did finally finish college, he still couldn't find anything he was particularly good at, so he went to law school. He left his family and everyone he knew in the south to go to law school in Nebraska, thinking that if he fell flat on his face, no one would be there to see it. It wasn't so much that he really even wanted to be a lawyer. It was just the corner he had painted himself into.

By 11 a.m. Dexter was in County Court with a legal pad and a new file folder to pick up the Donald Birch paper work and start building a client file. Dexter wanted to start reviewing the case before lunch. Then he would have time before the prelim to talk with the County Attorney about the case and visit with his client. The name "Donald Birch" just kept running through Dexter's head. It was not the name of any of the frequent fliers of the local criminal justice system. Still, Dexter knew that he knew that name somehow.

Donald Alan Birch was 73 years old. He was self-employed in "real estate." He was charged with three counts of first degree murder. Dexter did know Don Birch, he had known Don for as long as Dexter had lived in town. Don had been his first landlord when Dexter had moved to town.

Donald Birch had followed some relative to this part of Nebraska from Arkansas after finishing an eight-year stint in the Navy. No one recalled anymore what part of Arkansas he was from, nor did anyone recall the relative who had lived here first. But, once here, Don took a job in the maintenance department of one of the local factories that no longer existed. He took the money he had saved in the Navy and bought two houses. He lived in one while he fixed-up both. Then he rented the other house out and bought two more houses to fix-up and rent. After ten years, he was no longer working in the factory. He owned eight rental houses, four duplexes and an old motor lodge that rented rooms out by the week or the month. He had also married a local girl, a school teacher named Linda Heinemann, and they had three daughters. Linda was from one of the older families in the county. Her family wasn't rich, but they were respected and well known. Linda had continued to teach, and by the time she retired, she had taught about seventy percent of the county, including the sheriff, the county attorney and at least half of the courthouse staff. All three of Don and Linda's daughters had gone to college to become teachers. Only one of them was still teaching.

It had been a few years since Dexter had gotten his building and moved out of the duplex he had rented from Don. But, it was a small town and their paths crossed from time to time and they would exchange pleasantries.

Remembering all of this about Don only confused Dexter more. Why was a guy like Don Birch charged with three counts of first degree murder? And why in the Hell had

Dexter, of all attorneys, been appointed to represent Don? Looking back through the court filings, Dexter thought there must be some mistake.

Dexter turned to the Clerk Magistrate of the County Court who had handed him the complaint and court documents. "There must be a mistake in here somewhere."

"Nope, no mistake." The clerk said, eyebrows raised with a tight-lipped smile just to show how much she was enjoying Dexter's consternation. "The other public defenders both have conflicts in this case and Judge Anderson says you can handle the preliminary hearing. He says if Judge Ostergart wants to appoint special counsel once the case is in District Court, it can come out of his budget.

"Besides, rumor has it your client isn't going to live long enough to see a trial. That's why he killed them."

"Who did he kill?"

"Jesus, where have you been?" It was now the clerk's turn to show consternation as she put her fists on her hips and knitted her eyebrows.

"On vacation." Dexter shot back, a little irritated.

"Oh, right, that much needed break of yours. He killed his sons-in-law, all three of them."

Dexter opened the file and scoured the paperwork. Don had not posted bond, not surprisingly. Dexter decided to make the jail his next stop.

The jail was bigger than the county needed. That was by design. The jail made the county money by holding inmates for other counties and the feds. Dexter stood in the jail library waiting for an officer to bring in Donald Birch. It was about fifteen minutes into the lunch service and visiting a client at that time usually irritated the staff. But, they knew this was a special case and Dexter was normally good about respecting the jail routines and procedures. It also helped that he sent donuts or pizzas in to the jail staff at Christmas every year.

The twelve by twelve library was lined with bookshelves on three walls, filled with old paperback westerns, romance novels, Bibles, and AA books. Dexter sat at the lone table, situated in the center of the room and littered with magazines. He was trying to guess what Don might be reading to occupy himself when the door opened. Don Birch looked his age. He was about five-foot nine and maybe weighed a hundred and fifty pounds. His hair was still black on top and showed no signs of thinning. But, on the sides, where he wore it almost shorn, it was mostly grey. It was neatly combed, and it was obvious Don had shaved the night before or that morning. He had his orange jail shirt tucked into the elastic waist of his orange jail pants. Don was a man of habit and maintaining a particular bearing. Not having a belt to wear was almost certainly driving him crazy.

Right away Don smiled and started across the small room with his hand out to shake Dexter's. Clients, even those with far less serious charges were never this glad to see that Dexter would be their lawyer. But, this was going to be like no other case in Dexter's career up to this point and probably ever after.

"Boy, Dexter Smith, it is good to see a friendly face by golly." It came back to Dexter that this was how Don talked, all "Glad to see you," and "How are your friend?" It was hokey, but Dexter knew it was also genuine.

"Well, Don, it's good to see you too. But, I wish it were, you know, under better circumstances and all. You're in kind of a pickle here. I don't even know if I'm the right lawyer for you."

"Nah, that's what that prosecutor, Wilbur Pedersen said about you when I went to court before. But the judge said you would do fine and I told them both that I thought you would do a fine job too. I heard you were on vacation. You go to Arkansas?"

"Yes sir, for part of the trip."

"Yeah, you're from the north-east corner though, aren't you? My people are clear on the other side." Don paused, seeming to snap back into the reality of his situation. "So, anyway, what do we do now?"

"Look Don. I have always liked you and you were really good to me when I first got into town and needed a place to stay and all." Dexter had his hand on Don's shoulder now and was speaking calmly, but deliberately. "And, I really appreciate your confidence in me, I really do. But, you are facing some very serious charges here. The most serious. And, well, I'm not exactly Clarence Darrow."

"Who's that?" Don asked, pulling back a little.

"Well, he was a pretty famous defense lawyer.... I guess maybe I should say I'm not Perry Mason."

"Hell, I know that," Don said excitedly, throwing his hands half in the air. "He was just a t.v. lawyer, you're the real deal Dexter."

Dexter shook his head a little, embarrassed by the confidence Don was showing in him. "Look, I'm not some big, hotshot miracle worker lawyer, like O. J. had. Seventy percent of my practice is court appointed stuff. Get it? I'm a public defender. I'm more like a social worker sometimes than a regular lawyer. Don't get me wrong, I can get a hell of a deal for a DUI client or a drug addict charged with burglary, just trying to get cash for a quick fix. I may even get a judge to find reasonable doubt in a shop lifting trial or suppress a bad traffic stop. But, mostly, what I do is help people caught dead to rights, guilty as shit, get a deal." Dexter looked off to the side for a moment, taking a breath to find his next words. "I show them how to get some drug or alcohol counseling, to show that they are trying to change their ways, so they can get probation. I'm not a lawyer who represents someone charged with murder, much less someone charged with three counts of murder."

Don shook all this off. "I don't care, I like you, son. I trust you. I know you can do this stuff. Besides, I'm dying, so it don't really matter that much anyway what happens."

And there it was, confirmation of what Dexter had heard from the clerk magistrate. Dexter sat back, almost embarrassed to be relieved by what he was hearing. Don explained to Dexter that about the time Dexter was heading off on his vacation two weeks earlier, Don was at the hospital giving blood panels to try to figure out the dizziness and pain in his guts that wouldn't go away. And, a few days later, an endocrinology resident from Omaha called Don directly to tell him the news. Bypassing Don's local doctor, Mel Jones, the resident told Don that given the test results that included certain enzymes and blood sugar levels that Don and now Dexter didn't understand in the least, it was certain that Don had pancreatic cancer, probably advanced and maybe even spreading. Pancreatic cancer is bad, and Don should have gone right away to his family doctor to get set up with an oncologist. But, Don's mind raced to all the business he had to get in order. And all that started with his daughters.

"My wife and I just started talking about Debra, my middle daughter. Her husband, Scott, put her in the hospital about five years ago, when he had his drug problem. I wanted to kill him then. But, Debra stuck with him and he straightened out. Then, he started drinking last year and he got that DUI. I just worried what other bad habits would come back."

Dexter remembered when Scott Miller put his wife in the hospital. Scott had hired Dexter to represent him after he was referred to Dexter by John Miller, one of the other two attorneys with county contracts. John was Scott's cousin, and that wasn't the kind of case a lawyer wanted to represent a relative in. So, Dexter realized, that was one of the conflicts that landed Don's case in Dexter's lap now.

Scott was a motor head, but one with a head for business. He had owned a muffler and tire shop that he had built up himself. He was heavily into the local dirt track scene and spent most of his spare time working on racecars with his friends. It was probably around the track that he was introduced to meth. He hit rock bottom quick, and then he hit his wife, a lot. Dexter had gotten a serious domestic assault charge plead down to a misdemeanor, and Scott spent the next year on probation after doing a stint of inpatient drug treatment.

The scandal had nearly cost his wife her teaching job. It did cost him his business. So Scott went to work in the service department of his wife's brother-in-law's car dealership. Scott had worked his way up to manager of the service department, until a year ago when he got drunk and wrecked a dealership car he was driving at the time. He lost that job.

The last Dexter had heard, Scott was getting by doing work in the shop behind his house. Dexter would soon learn that it was in that shop that Scott was killed. To Dexter's recollection, Scott and Debra did not have kids. That was probably for the best.

"I don't know for sure why I went to see Scott or what I intended to do. I didn't plan to kill him." Dexter thought that Don sounded rehearsed when he told his story. Dexter chalked it up to Don having over a week in jail to sit and think about what he would say when given the chance. "I just got to his shop and there was no one else around. He was under that Cadillac, front wheel stripped down to the spindle and up on a floor jack. Not even a jack-stand under it. Scott was never careless like that. It was too easy. I don't even know what he was doing under there. I doubt he even knew I was there. I just walked in, saw the situation and I grabbed the handle of the floor-jack and turned. That car came down. His legs twitched a little. And that was it. I just walked out."

Plainly stunned by what he had just heard, Dexter suddenly realized Don had stopped talking and had an embarrassed look on his face. They may be getting into things Dexter didn't need to hear about, at least not yet.

"OK Don, we will need to get into all of this at some point. But we need to go slow. There may be some things I don't need to know. It doesn't mean I don't care." Again, Dexter looked off to the side and took a breath while he searched for words. "Today is your preliminary hearing. We don't do anything but listen to the deputies testifying about what they THINK they know and what they think they can prove." Dexter and Don kept their eyes fixed on each other's, Dexter was speaking almost rhythmically now, punctuating each sentence with a dramatic pause. "I also need to finish reading the reports and I need to talk to Wilbur Pedersen. We can also address bond at the hearing, but they don't have to give you one for these charges. If they do, it will be about a million dollars, cash.

"After the hearing you can also tell me who I can and can't talk to about your case. You may want me to talk to your wife, probably not your daughters. I don't want to talk to more than one or two people besides you. I hope they saved your lunch. I'm sorry I interrupted it." Dexter crouched to stand as he extended his hand to Don.

Don took Dexter's hand, also starting to stand, and smiled. "That's ok, they served me first and I was done before you came in. I can't stand to eat much with this pain in my gut anyway."

After hitting the intercom button, a jailer came to the door to take Don back to his housing pod and Dexter showed himself out through the series of automatic doors that were being operated by an anonymous hand in a control room somewhere filled with video screens.

Dexter went back to his office and started reading the arrest affidavit and the main body of the investigative reports that he had so far. The arrest affidavit was short, to the point: *Roy Musgrave's body was found in his office at his car dealership at about 9:45 p.m. on the night of the killings by the night janitors. He had suffered extensive blunt force trauma to the head, face and upper body. He was found face down in a pool of blood with the back of his head opened and brains exposed. A large wooden mallet found later that night in the bed of Donald Birch's truck was covered with blood and hair. A member of the janitorial crew, a tenant of Donald Birch, reported that Donald Birch's truck was pulling away from the dealership as the crew arrived that evening.*

As the 911 operator was finishing up the broadcast of this news, Sheriff Dennis Coffee was getting a call on his cell phone from Jeff Hays' neighbor, Joe Freisen, that he had just heard several pops coming from next door that sounded like firecrackers or a .22. Coffee recognized the connection between Roy Musgrave and Jeff Hays right off and sent his chief deputy, Bob Anderson, to the Hays residence while the Sheriff headed to the car dealership to take charge of that scene. Anderson found Jeff Hays slumped in a recliner with what appeared to be several small caliber bullet holes in his torso just before Linda Hays entered the house with her bowling ball.

Sheriff Coffee turned the dealership scene over to the State Patrol investigators as soon as they arrived to assist, and went to the Hays residence. The Sheriff and Chief Deputy were then able to calm Linda Hays down with the assistance of her mother, Linda Birch, who had just arrived. Then, with the situation somewhat under control, the sheriff sent Bob Anderson out to account for Scott Miller and Donald Birch.

Bob Anderson's first stop was at Scott Miller's house, two blocks away. Debra Miller answered the door and said that she had fallen asleep in front of the t.v. after getting home from work and had not seen her husband yet. She was nervous that a deputy was there looking for her husband, which was understandable given his history. She and Anderson went to the garage out back, where the light was still on, to find Scott's legs sticking out from under a Cadillac along with what would prove to be streams and pools of his blood.

Dexter stopped himself there. This was going to be a lot to digest. He already realized that everyone in town but he knew the whole story or some version of it. The story would have made its rounds and died out a little while he was on vacation. Then they would have recirculated after the funerals, which may not have happened yet because of autopsies. Dexter wondered if there had ever been a murder in the county's history, much less a triple murder.

Dexter hated to admit it, but as serious as all of this was looking, he hoped Don Birch's death by cancer would come quick. It would be best for all involved. Bury all four of them and move on.

Dexter looked back through the end of the reports enough to get that Bob Anderson had easily gotten a motive and confession from Don Birch and that Wilbur Pedersen, County Attorney and therefore, under Nebraska law, County Coroner, had made his rounds to make the deaths official and get the bodies to the M.E. in Lincoln for autopsy. What a night and next day that must have been for everyone.

2

Before becoming County Attorney, Wilbur Pedersen had been his father's Deputy County Attorney. It was all part of a family business that included three thousand acres of farm ground, two cattle feeding operations, and a haying company. When Wilbur's father had first become County Attorney, it was a position that took very little time, leaving him mostly to his private legal practice and management of his family's farming enterprises. The position had changed since then. Wilbur spent so much of his time being County Attorney that he had little time for his own private practice, which consisted of his own family's legal work and the tax and estate work of a handful of the biggest landowners in the area. Wilbur's younger brothers ran the farming and feeding operations. And, Wilbur usually had two deputy county attorneys on staff to do the most tedious of the county's legal work. Those positions turned over every couple of years, and were usually filled by recent law school graduates who only stuck with Wilbur until they got enough experience to move elsewhere. This suited Wilbur.

Rumor had it that as soon as Wilbur's son, who was finishing law school, was ready to take over as county attorney, Wilbur would run for the Third District US House Seat. Wilbur had worked hard for the Republican Party, not just in the county, but throughout the state. Wilbur had made friends and accumulated favors. There was no reason to think he wouldn't win such an election.

Wilbur Pedersen's family had helped to settle the area after the Civil War and they had done very well for themselves. Pedersens mattered around here. And, if Wilbur were ever to forget this, his mother would remind him. While Wilbur's father was a Pedersen by accident of birth, Mildred Pedersen had become one by shear self-determination. It was a determination that stunned her husband the first time they sat next to each other in Sunday school as children, and left him somewhat stunned until the day she buried him.

Mildred Pedersen came from another family that settled the county. Her grandfather had been the first Lutheran minister in the area. Her father had been a banker, a real estate developer, and a state senator. Mildred herself had studied sacred music in college, knowing that while an education was expected of her, taking any kind of job would be beneath her once she became Mrs. Charles Pedersen.

Besides fulfilling her duty of perpetuating the Pedersen bloodline and playing organ at her church, Mildred was something of a self-appointed cultural leader in the community. Mildred was best known for her annual trips to Lincoln to attend the big fundraisers for public television and public radio. Three years in a row she had been the highest bidder in the auction for Bob Ross original paintings, the ones he painted on the show. One of the three paintings hung in the parlor of the Lutheran Church, one in the main branch of the county library and the third in her own dining room.

When Dexter Smith got to Lee Ho Fook's Chinese Restaurant fifteen minutes before the usual lunch crowd, he found himself face to face with Mildred Pedersen who had just finished an early lunch with her son.

"Hello, Mrs. Pedersen."

"Hello," she answered back, smiling stiffly. She gave every indication that she was not quite sure who he was exactly or how she was expected to know him. But, the fact was, she knew exactly who he was. He was an outsider, an interloper, not even a Nebraskan. He was from somewhere down south. And he had had the impudence at some point in his life to go to law school and become a lawyer. Her husband had been a lawyer. Her son was a lawyer. Her grandson would be a lawyer. Being a lawyer was supposed to mean something. Something more than this man standing in front of her in a cheap hopsack blazer and Dickies. He was clearly not the same kind of lawyer as her lawyers.

Wilbur, still paying the bill, turned from the counter to see Dexter. He joined Dexter and Mildred at the door, kissed his mother on the cheek and asked to be excused from her company to discuss the afternoon's hearing with Dexter.

"Dex, the prelim this afternoon,"

"I can't waive it, I have to have a prelim on a murder case." Dexter said half over his shoulder, making his way to his usual table with Wilbur in tow.

"You're damn right you do. Just don't continue it. We need to have it today and get it bound up to District Court. Ask for a bond reduction today and I won't object. Sheriff Coffee has the ankle monitor from the probation office ready for your client and Judge Anderson is on board with all this."

"He's going to get out? You and the Judge are going to let someone out on an ankle monitor? You have never agreed to that before."

"We've never had a defendant with a medical condition that could bankrupt the county before either. He stays in jail, the county pays for his medical. Your client needs to get out of jail and see a doctor and get his affairs in order. He's got nowhere to go, no reason to run. The medical examiner has released the bodies and the funerals are going to start in a couple of days. Let's get him out while everyone is talking about the funerals. Let's run everything else by the book until he's gone too." They were now settling into Dexter's usual table at the back of the restaurant, near the kitchen.

"This also goes above and beyond your contract. So, keep up with your hours on this one. You go over your expected hours, the county pays you for them. You need help with this one, tell Judge Ostergart you want the Commission on Public Advocacy appointed to help.

"We want to do all of this by the book, until it dies its own natural death, then we put it behind us and move on."

Dexter was still trying to absorb all of this. Don didn't look great, but he didn't look like he was dying to Dexter. But, what did Dexter know? The waitress brought Dexter a can of Diet Dr. Pepper. It was not on the menu. Dexter bought it himself and kept it in the restaurant for lunch. It was the only time Dexter drank Diet Dr. Pepper. The rest of the time he drank Diet Coke or coffee. She sat the can on his table and asked if he would be having the chicken or the lo mein. He always had one of those two for lunch. He never ordered dinner in the evenings, he just ate what the owner's family was eating. It was never something from the menu and he was rarely sure what it was. He always liked it.

Dexter studied Wilbur and all he was saying. He could see that Wilbur was in the driver's seat on this case and would try to stay there. Dexter knew that would get interesting up in District Court where Judge Ostergart had the temerity to run his own courtroom. Dexter didn't mind what Wilbur was doing though. He appreciated it, because Wilbur would not want to push a defense attorney around in a case like this or look like he was trying to railroad someone into a conviction. Wilbur would also not want to use a murder case to grandstand. In places like New York a prosecutor with political aspirations made a name for himself going after the bad guys in high profile cases. In places like Nebraska people wanted to believe there were no bad guys. If Wilbur was truly going to run for the US House one day, he was going to get there because there were no problems in his community, everything was perfect here, because of men like Wilbur. And, people around here would send him to Washington to make the rest of the country as safe and boring.

So, Wilbur Pedersen probably hated this situation as much as anyone; with the possible exception of Don Birch's family. Wilbur wanted all of this to go as smoothly as possible. No drama. If Don Birch lived long enough to go to trial, twelve registered voters would sit in a jury box and see how professional, thorough, calm and conscientious Wilbur Pedersen was. There would be a conviction and no grounds for appeal. Wilbur wouldn't do anything underhanded; and he would make sure Dexter didn't screw anything up.

"I am sorry you got stuck with this Dexter, I don't need the headache of it all either. But, John Miller is related to one of the victims and Tom McWilliams can't do it because he's going to be up to his neck in Roy Musgrave's trust and estate. Hell, Tom's going to have to practically prosecute Don in probate court, then I will probably have to put Tom on the stand to prove up on Don's motive for killing Roy." Tom was the best lawyer around. It was no surprise he was Roy Musgrave's lawyer. Tom did pretty much every kind of law and did it well; he had even once handled a capital murder case. He had also done more than his share of appellate work and everyone who knew about such things knew that when Daniel Ostergart retired from the District Court bench, Tom McWilliams was the likely candidate to take his place.

It was the only real reason Tom did public defender work. Most criminal defendants couldn't afford to hire a lawyer, but a lawyer who wants to be a District Court Judge needs that criminal law experience and to stay up on it. Tom's contract with the county was for the more serious felonies only.

Dexter still had questions. "I know who Roy Musgrave is, or was. I know he owns the car dealership here and another one somewhere. I know he is rich and I know he is an asshole. I represent people who work for him. But, that is as close as I get to the guy. So, what does Tom McWilliams have to prove-up for you? And does this mean that I can't go asking Tom for advice like I usually do when I'm in over my head?"

"Any advice Tom wants to give you is between you two, if he is comfortable helping you, which I doubt he will be. But, if he does help you out any, it needs to stay between the two of you. I don't even want to know about it. I especially don't want to know about it.

"As for what Tom is dealing with now. Well, Roy Musgrave didn't own two car dealerships. His father owned two car dealerships; and put them in a trust for Roy. Roy gets a divorce, his wife doesn't get half. Roy just gets a good salary to run the business, she would probably get some temporary support, but that is it, she wouldn't even get child support because their kids are in college now. Even their house is owned by the trust, so she can't get anything from that. Now that Roy's dead. The trust dissolves, and the proceeds will be divided among her and the kids, unless she was involved in Roy's death.

"Marcia, Roy's wife, Don's daughter, has M.S. Roy didn't want to deal with that. Roy liked to party. Roy liked his girls on the side. Roy didn't like people talking behind his back about what a rotten son-of-a-bitch he was for treating poor Marcia like this. So, the kids are off at college, Roy was probably about to divorce Marcia, throw a little money at her and she moves east to be closer to her doctors and the kids who are in college. Roy was about to be a free man.

"But, Roy is now dead, the trust dissolves, and Marcia and the kids are very well-off. That is Don's motive for killing Roy, and Marcia could be complicit in the murder. That is what Tom will have to show in probate court and testify to if we go to trial. So, helping you could put Tom in a real bind." Wilbur excused himself to get back to his office and let Dexter digest the information along with his lunch.

Dexter ate his chicken and thought about Tom.

Tom McWilliams was not just the best lawyer in town, he was also a good man and had taken a liking to Dexter when Dexter had first moved to town. Tom helped

Dexter get his own contract with the county, taking the less serious criminal cases as well as child support enforcement cases and juvenile cases. Tom had also referred cases to Dexter over the years when he was too busy himself to take on new clients. And, most of all, he was never too busy to give Dexter a case citation or point him in the right procedural direction when Dexter was lost in the weeds. Representing Donald Birch on three counts of murder made Dexter nervous. Not being able to go to Tom McWilliams for help made Dexter sick to his stomach.

****

The small County Courtroom was packed for the hearing with a few reporters, law enforcement, and about half of the courthouse staff who had been able to sneak over. Dexter also spotted some women he guessed were Don's wife and daughters.

Wilbur first called Sheriff Dennis Coffee to the stand. After a stint as an Army Ranger, Coffee had worked for small local law enforcement agencies throughout Western Nebraska and Wyoming before coming back home to run for sheriff eight years before.

Once on the stand, Coffee laid out the crime scenes, how and when they were discovered and what various deputies, investigators, and state troopers did at each of the scenes. He took about twenty minutes. Dexter had no questions for the sheriff on cross examination.

Then, Chief Deputy Sheriff Bob Anderson took the stand. He testified as to how he had learned of the crimes, how the sheriff had directed him to go to Jeff Hays' house and then Scott Miller's. He explained what he saw and did at each location.

Next, Bob explained how he went to Don Birch's house and which deputies accompanied him, how he approached Don and told Don he needed to be questioned down at the station. He said Don did not seem to be surprised at the deputies' presence or the news that his three sons-in-law were dead. Bob then testified that he took a quick look around the house, with Don's permission, while Don was being placed into Bob's patrol unit by one of the other deputies. Don had been told that he was going to be placed into cuffs as standard procedure for "officer safety."

Then, Bob Anderson told the Court how Don Birch had confessed everything in the patrol car on the way to the sheriff's office and how, once at the sheriff's office, in the interview room with cameras and audio running, Don wrote out a statement that was verbatim what he had told Bob in the car.

Bob Anderson had been a cop for almost forty years. He had been the top investigator at the sheriff's office for eighteen of those years, until Coffee took office and moved Bob to Chief Deputy. Bob was still, hands down, the best criminal investigator in the department, which was why Coffee had called him out the night of the murders and had put Bob in charge of all scenes, which should have been an investigator's job.

Dexter took all of this in and scribbled notes the whole time Bob was testifying. And, eventually, it occurred to Dexter; it was odd, but Dexter was sure of it. Bob Anderson was nervous. Bob listened carefully to every leading question that Wilbur asked him, rolled each question over in his head before giving a deliberate and thoughtful answer. He did not answer a single question or go into any important details without first reviewing his notepad which was in front of him.

After eighteen years as the lead investigator, Bob had testified at more preliminary hearings than the rest of the sheriff's office combined, and that included the sheriff.

Dexter had learned what to ask or not ask a cop at a preliminary hearing by watching Bob Anderson stare down defense attorneys from the stand and spit sullen, cocky answers back at their questions. This was not the usual Bob Anderson on the witness stand. And, while Bob's testimony was deliberate and covering all the bases, Dexter also noticed an unusual tone of irritation that Wilbur Pedersen was taking with Bob.

After forty minutes of testifying, Pedersen was done with Bob. When the Judge offered Dexter his chance at cross examination, Bob gave Dexter a look that was half "please don't" and half "don't you even think about it you piss-ant." Dexter declined the opportunity. He had learned long ago not to agitate a sick dog.

The State rested, and Dexter Smith had no evidence to put on, it was a prelim, the state's show, not his. The State submitted the case without a closing argument. Dexter made an impotent argument about the lack of evidence regarding Don Birch's connection to Jeff Hays' shooting and how Scott Miller's death sounded like an accident entirely, except for the part where Don confessed. Dexter felt silly saying all of this, but after not crossing either witness or putting on any evidence of his own, he felt he needed to do something.

The Judge gave Dexter a nonplussed look over his glasses that made Dexter realize that doing and saying nothing would have been much, much better. Judge Anderson then banged his gavel and bound the case over to the District Court for arraignment and trial.

The matter of bond was then taken up. "Mr. Pedersen, I will now address bond. Does the State have any special concerns, or should the bond be set at one million dollars, cash?"

"Your Honor, this is a most unusual case. The Defendant has very strong ties to the community, as well as serious medical needs that the county is not equipped to deal with in the jail. We would therefore not object to a defense motion to have Mr. Birch released without posting bond under the condition that he wear an electronic monitoring devise at all times and not leave this county except to go to medical appointments after giving the Sheriff's Office notice of the appointment twenty-four hours in advance."

"Hearing no objection from the State, Mr. Smith, your motion is granted." It was such an eloquent and ingeniously crafted motion, Dexter wished he had actually made it.

Don Birch was then given a District Court arraignment date in six weeks. He was taken out of the courtroom by the jail staff and back to the jail to process his release.

Dexter turned to a woman sitting behind him he was fairly sure was Don's wife, Linda. He nodded and smiled. He was not entirely sure who the women with her were. He thought at first that they were Don and Linda's daughters, but then he realized that would make them the victims' widows. What would their daughters do, support the man who killed their husbands, or turn their backs on their mother and dying father at such a desperate time? This case was only going to get weirder.

3

Dexter had planned his vacation so that he would be back to work on a Thursday, work two days, and have a weekend. It was four forty-eight Thursday afternoon. He was ready for the weekend. He walked back to his office, threw Don's file on the desk, locked the office and walked two blocks to his usual bar.

There had been a bar where The Pawnee Club was housed for over a hundred years. The name just changed with each new owner. Sam Hagan had owned the place for longer than Dexter had been in town. Most people thought about the Cheyenne or the Sioux or even the Arapaho when they thought about Native Americans and Nebraska history. Being an amateur Nebraska Historian, Sam knew that the Pawnee had fought those other tribes for the U.S. Army and the first white settlers, only to have their help forgotten and their character besmirched by Hollywood. So, he named his bar after them to make amends.

Dexter looked forward to catching up with Sam after his two weeks away. He made his way to the center of the bar, where the waitress station and cash register were. Sam had the walk-in cooler door propped open and was stocking the small beer coolers behind the bar, but stopped when he realized Dexter had come in. "Hey Dex. Love to hear about your trip and your first big day back, as soon as I finish up here." He said all this while opening Dexter a bottle of Busch Light. The smile on his face told Dexter that Sam already knew quite a bit about his first big day back.

"No hurry Sam. I need to get a few of these in me before I talk about anything. Some first day back."

"Well, Mr. Smith. How the hell are ya?" It was Pat Blocker, just to Dexter's right, watching the Keno board above him and drinking his usual amaretto and Sprite. Dexter had walked right past him without noticing him.

"How ya doing Pat?"

"Well, pretty good. Except one of my bosses killed another one of my bosses, so I'm just doing my Burger Hut job now. Plus, they were both pretty good guys. And the whole thing sucks." Dexter knew right away that Pat was talking about Don Birch and his son-in-law, Jeff Hays. Pat and a friend of his, Teddy Pickrell, did odd jobs for both men around the rental properties they owned. Pat might be just the guy to shed light on a few things.

****

Pat Blocker was in his early thirties. He received partial social security for a developmental disability, so he was limited in the number of hours he could work a week at a regular job. He was also the sole beneficiary of an irrevocable trust his grandfather had set up for him after selling the family livestock auction business. Pat and his father were both only children, then Pat's parents were killed in a car accident when Pat was still in high school. So, grandpa, getting too old to run the business and knowing that Pat would always be too young, sold the business and his house and Pat's parents' house and put everything in the trust for Pat, making Wilbur Pedersen the trustee.

Pat and grandpa moved into an apartment above the diner two doors down from The Pawnee Club. When grandpa died about five years later, Wilbur Pedersen became Pat's guardian and conservator as well as the trustee of the trust. Pat never left the apartment; the trust paid the rent and basic utilities and the running tab at the diner where Pat took all his meals.

Pat's former best friend and now arch enemy was Teddy Pickrell. They had had every class together in school since fourth grade. As soon as Grandpa Blocker died, Teddy moved into the apartment above the café with Pat. And, that was when the trouble began. It wasn't serious trouble, just stupid alcohol fueled pranks. The problem was, Wilbur

27

Pedersen was Pat's guardian and conservator, so every time Pat got cited into court or arrested, Wilbur had to recuse himself and the county had to pay for a special prosecutor, usually a deputy county attorney from a neighboring county. It had started to get expensive, and embarrassing.

So, when Pat was arrested because Teddy had dared him to piss in the open window of a state trooper's cruiser, Judge Anderson declared that Pat was no longer in need of a guardian/conservator and Wilbur turned over duties as trustee to the president of the local bank that held the trust. Without a guardian, Pat promised to put most of his social security check in the trust and he kept the rest along with what he made at his part-time jobs to do with as he pleased.

Along with rent, utilities, and meals at the diner, the trust bought Pat new clothes a couple of times a year. The trust did not pay Pat's tab at The Pawnee Club or pay for the meals Teddy ate with Pat at the diner. A dispute over these last two facts came to a head one day between Pat and the banker and very nearly got Pat barred from the very bank that managed his trust. Fortunately for all involved, Dexter happened to be in the bank making a rare deposit into his client trust account. Dexter intervened and calmed Pat down and escorted him out of the bank. Not only did Dexter and Pat both frequent The Pawnee Club, but Dexter was often appointed to represent Pat and/or Teddy when they were charged in their drunken escapades. This is why, despite the long-standing relationship between the Blocker and Pedersen families, Pat always thought of Dexter as his lawyer rather than Wilbur. It was an attorney/client relationship that Pat could comprehend.

Not long after Pat was declared competent to make his own decisions in life, he realized one new liberty that had until then been denied him, internet shopping. Though he had never been offered a credit card, and didn't know how to go about getting one on his own, Pat somehow figured out that he could get a disposable debit card, load it up with cash and shop online with it. The first thing he did was to go on Amazon and buy three hundred and sixty-six different Bruce Lee t-shirts. One for each day of the year, including one that would only be worn every four years on February 29. This became a hot topic for the local businessmen on Main Street who had coffee together at the diner every morning, after one had heard the story from Sam Hagan. The most controversial issue, which was discussed heatedly for two days among the group was whether there could actually be that many "different" Bruce Lee t-shirts. Finally, a young insurance salesman took the time to look on Amazon and confirmed to the group the next day that there were, in fact, a seemingly infinite number of Bruce Lee t-shirts once one considered all the options for not only the graphics on the shirt, but the choice of color that each graphic came on as well as the options for short-sleeve, long-sleeve, or tank.

Then, because there is no real confidentiality in a small town when it comes to fiduciary duties, all the other businessmen spent the coffee breaks of the next two mornings harassing the banker for not reimbursing Pat for the t-shirts from the trust. In the end, he did reimburse Pat, just to shut his friends up. And it was justifiable because the trust would never have to buy Pat another t-shirt for as long as he lived. There were simply too many of the shirts for them all to wear out, even if Pat let Teddy wear one of the shirts, which was rarely and only on special occasions.

The funny thing was, the shirts fit Teddy perfectly but were too small for Pat. Pat was about five feet six inches tall and two hundred fifty pounds. He was easily a triple X shirt size. Pat normally bought his clothes in the store, and just tried them on without ever paying attention to the size. So, when he bought his Bruce Lee shirts online, rather than look at the tag of the shirt he had on, he recalled that his grandpa ordered his clothes from Sears and Roebuck and always ordered extra-large. That was back when Pat was about fourteen. The sad result was that the Bruce Lee shirts were too tight, and barely covered Pat's naval.

By the time Dexter had finished his third Busch Light, he was ready to tell Sam and Pat about his vacation, but it had been uneventful compared to the short time he had been back, so he had already forgotten most of it. What Dexter really wanted to do was get Sam and Pat talking about what all had gone on in town regarding Don Birch while he had been gone.

Dexter set his empty bottle out to the back edge of the bar and as Sam reached in the cooler for another one, Dexter offered to get Pat's next amaretto and Sprite. He didn't offer to get Sam anything because Sam only drank coffee and that was free. About that time, Teddy Pickrell walked in. Until then, Dexter and Pat had been the only patrons in the place. Dexter told Sam he would be paying for Teddy's PBR and Teddy thanked Dexter for this as he moved coolly past Pat and took a place at the bar two seats past Dexter's left. In the last six months, Teddy and Pat had not spoken and Teddy had moved back in with his family. Dexter picked up on the sudden coolness in the room and gave Sam a wincing look that Sam returned with a nod and an eye roll. The fissure between Pat and Teddy was wearing on everyone who dealt with the two on a regular basis. It was all over Gracie June Parker.

Gracie June was a woman of substantial girth and a former classmate of Teddy and Pat. She had lived with an aunt in Omaha since high school but had moved back to town a year or so earlier. She had tried working at the Burger Hut with Pat and Teddy. But work did not suit her and there had been complaints from customers and other staff about her hygiene.

Gracie lived in a singlewide in a trailer park on the edge of town with her older brother. It had not taken her long to learn about Pat's steady stream of support from the trust, and an attraction soon arose. Because Gracie June was female, and she was willing to talk to Pat, the attraction was mutual.

Soon, Pat was spending a good deal of time at Gracie June's, which only irritated the shit out of her brother, Harley. Harley's real name was Wendel, but he did not allow people to call him that. He liked "Harley" because of the motorcycle, even though all he had ever had all his life were rat bikes and he had never even sat on a Harley Davidson.

Harley was always suggesting that Pat and Gracie June go to Pat's place. But Pat didn't like the familiar way Teddy talked to Gracie June around their apartment.

Then, Harley became aware of Pat's steady income stream, as well as the fascination Pat and Teddy had with Bruce Lee and martial arts. So, Harley decided that given his own training in martial arts and self-defense, which he had gotten from going half way through Marine Corps. Basic training, he was more than qualified to give them the training they had always wanted but had always alluded them.

Now, Pat and Teddy had taken an interest in martial arts in general, and Bruce Lee in particular, when they were in the seventh grade, after spending an entire Saturday afternoon in Pat's family room watching a Bruce Lee marathon. When they got back to school on Monday, they found a book on Bruce Lee in the school library. This became the first book that either had ever read from start to finish, and this did not go unnoticed by their resource teacher. Not realizing what she was about to unleash, the teacher ordered every book on Bruce Lee and the martial arts she could locate on Pat and Teddy's grade level, and two levels above.

Pat and Teddy read all these books, from start to finish. By the end of the school year, their reading comprehension scores had spiked, but so had their school incident reports from attempting to put to practice what they had read. For better or worse, the nearest martial arts schools were fifty miles away. And so, Pat and Teddy's martial arts expertise would never be anything but theoretical.

But, now, after all these years, there was Harley. And it would only cost them twenty dollars each for an hour lesson every Saturday. On the first day, Pat showed up wearing a yellow one-piece track suit like Bruce Lee had worn in his last movie, The Game of Death. Of course, it had also been ordered online and was a couple of sizes too small and gave Pat camel toe. Teddy wore cut-offs and a plain white tank-top undershirt. No matter how Teddy had begged that morning, Pat would not let him wear a Bruce Lee t-shirt.

Harley had of course forgotten about the karate class and had to be roused from a sound sleep induced largely by the case of Keystone he had drunk the night before. He took the forty dollars, told his pupils to warm up by running four laps around the trailer court, and went back inside to lay down on the couch.

The trailer park was not that big, but Teddy and Pat were seriously out of shape. It was more than forty minutes later that Teddy was knocking on the door of the trailer. Harley came out with half a Keystone in his hand, starting to feel better. Teddy had now sprawled himself across the hood of a junk car moldering next to the trailer and Pat was cutting through the middle of the park, right through people's lots, holding his side, to get back up to the trailer. He had only managed two and a half laps.

"You disgusting, out of shape shit dogs! What makes either of you think that you are worthy of becoming martial artists like me and Bruce Lee? I'm not going to waste any more of my time on the two of you!"

"But we paid you" protested Teddy, now back on his feet. Pat was shaking his head in agreement with Teddy but had not gotten enough breath back to protest himself.

"Alright, you have fifteen minutes left I guess. The first thing you have to learn in the martial arts is how to take an ass beating like a man and not cry."

32

And with that, Harley delivered a swift kick to Teddy's balls and an elbow to the side of Pat's chin, causing both to crumple to the ground writhing. By the time they had both recovered and were back on their feet, the class had run ten minutes over and Harley insisted that each owed him five more dollars. They both promised to bring an extra five dollars to the following week's lesson.

Classes went on every Saturday until Teddy was as good at crazy gluing wounds shut as the ER doctor who had started to ask too many questions after seeing Teddy and Pat three Saturdays in a row. Finally, Chief Deputy Bob Anderson figured out what was going on and decided to put a stop to the nonsense before someone got seriously hurt.

Bob started off by having a long talk with Harley. Only, Bob made sure to call Harley by his given name, starting about every fourth sentence with "Now, Wendel." Bob was pretty sure Harley had gotten the message. Then, Bob moved on to Pat and Teddy. He told them that if they wanted to learn some martial arts techniques, they could come hold pads for the deputies when they had to recertify in self-defense. Bob had decided that number one, the deputies would not do too much damage to the pair, and number two, if anyone was going to knock Pat and Teddy around any, the deputies had earned the right to after putting up with them for so many years.

Soon after all this took place, and before any deputies needed to recertify in self-defense, Pat and Teddy's friendship was shaken to its core and Teddy had to find new digs after all the years in Pat's apartment. Gracie June Parker had announced that she was pregnant, but before Pat could wipe the silly grin off his face and get on one knee to propose marriage to her, Gracie June confessed that there were more than a couple potential fathers, including Teddy Pickrell.

Harley, much quicker than his sister in thought processes could not believe she had confessed this so quickly. It took him some time to calm down and explain to her why it would be beneficial to let Pat think he was the father, given his financial situation, even if he weren't.

As soon as Gracie's social services worker learned of the pregnancy, child support enforcement was notified, and child protective services was put on alert to check on the mother and child as soon as the child was born.

Through careful questioning by child support before the child was born, it was learned that the list of putative fathers included not only Teddy and Pat, but someone known only to Gracie June as "Spider" and another fellow known to Gracie June as "Spider's Brother."

It was further determined that conception probably coincided with the county fair and that Spider and Spider's Brother were transients in town with the carnival that worked the county fair. As word spread and people started recalling who all was in town for the fair and piecing all of that with the descriptions Gracie June gave of Spider, Spider's Brother, and their tattoos, it was decided that the two were most likely a couple of fellows working the carnival who some took to be Pacific Islanders of some sort. In fact, Sam Hagan was sure he had served them beers at The Pawnee Club while they were in town and that one of them had mentioned something about Samoa.

When Gracie June's daughter was born, it was apparent to everyone that Spider or Spider's Brother was the father. Right away Harley's irritation with his sister went away, realizing that even Pat would have never thought this was his child. Or, it could have just been love that melted away Harley's irritation. To the surprise of the case worker who followed the three Parkers home from the hospital, it was clear that Harley was taking very good care of his niece and making sure that Gracie June was too.

Despite the revelation that neither was the father of Gracie June's child, the friendship of Pat and Teddy had not repaired itself. It was a situation that was irritating the pure piss out of Sam Hagan. Like it or not they were two of his best customers. And, like it or not, he had become a de facto father to the pair, a responsibility he had until recent events shared with Don Birch and Jeff Hays. Jeff's death at Don's hands had weighed heavily on Pat and Teddy, and only made the tension between the two worse.

Sam and Dexter both felt uneasy as Pat and Teddy sat at the bar without acknowledging each other. Suddenly, Teddy turned to Dexter and said "So, Mr. Smith, I just heard them talking about you on the radio. You're gonna be Don Birch's lawyer, heh. They said you didn't say too much in court. I sure hope you can help Don."

"You just don't worry about that Teddy." Sam stepped in, "He can't talk about that stuff and you know that. Besides, I doubt if he even wants to talk about it in here. How would you like for us to ask you a bunch of questions about flipping burgers and making breakfast burritos when you come in here after a long day?" This was of course far from the truth. Dexter wanted insight on his new case from anyone willing to give it but was now feeling too sheepish to admit it.

"Hell, I don't mind talking shop." Teddy shot back at Sam. "I love my job. Especially since the boss started making sure that I don't ever get scheduled to work with you-know-who, down at the end of the bar." Teddy rolled his eyes and indicated Pat's direction with his thumb.

"Funny, I enjoy work a lot more too these days" was Pat's reply.

And, from there it went downhill. For no reason but to antagonize, Teddy took the conversation in a whole new direction. "You know, Sam, I've spent a lot of my life reading the works of Bruce Lee and studying his Jeet-Kun-Do, but lately I've been studying up on Ed Parker's American style of Kempo karate. I think it may be a much better form for the American body-type. Besides, if it was good enough for Elvis, it is good enough for me."

This brought Pat to his feet and halfway to where Teddy was sitting. Sure, Ed Parker had his place in martial arts lore. He helped launch Bruce Lee's career. But the Monkees had discovered Jimmi Hendrix and that sure as hell didn't make them the superior rock-n-roll act.

Teddy was now on his feet too, face to face with Pat, they were right behind Dexter who was turning around and starting to wish he were still in Court with Don Birch. Sam was on his way around the bar, but not too quickly.

"You don't know jack shit about Ed Parker or Kempo-karate."

"I know plenty about Sensei Ed Parker." Teddy shot back. "We used to be drinking buddies down at the Bad-Mother-Fuckers' Club."

As soon as Teddy said this, Pat threw a punch to Teddy's throat that made everyone freeze. Pat looked as surprised as Teddy; and Dexter and Sam looked even more surprised than the other two. They were all temporarily frozen, especially Teddy, who was now a very interesting shade of plum from the neck up.

Teddy stood there, holding his throat, staring ahead at Pat's chest, or maybe through Pat's chest, at nothing really. Slowly, Teddy let out a low, throaty whine and tears started to streak down his cheek as the whine grew louder. Pat started to cry too. But, as Pat reached out to Teddy, Teddy shoved the heal of his palm into Pat's face and as Pat staggered back, Teddy delivered a kick to Pat's balls, just like the one Harley had given Teddy at that first karate lesson.

Dexter and Sam were then between the two, like two grown men breaking up a fight between a couple of fifth graders. Sam, during all the action had somehow managed to fill a bar towel with ice and was holding it to Pat's bleeding nose. Dexter was holding Teddy in an upright position, trying to keep his airway open while Teddy regained his ability to breathe.

As the situation calmed, it was time for Sam's face to redden. "I have had enough of this shit and it stops right now. I have put up with a hell of a lot from you two for longer than I can remember, and a hell of a lot longer than I ever should have. But, this is too much. Pat, I know what Teddy did with Gracie June was wrong and he should be ashamed. Teddy, you know Goddamn good and well it was wrong too. You don't do what you did to a friend, much less your best friend, much less the only real friend you have ever had and will ever have. And Pat, like it or not, Teddy is probably the best and only real friend you will ever have, even though he let you down and was a complete shit this one time.

"Now, I don't care that the two of you spend most of your pay checks in here. What the two of you spend in here a month together won't even pay my electric bill." This was a lie. Sam had actually calculated it once, and what they spent in the bar a month did pay his electric bill. "Now, this shit is going to stop. Right now. I am supposed to call the cops right now, and I am supposed to cut you both off and ban you from the place. But I'm not going to.

"But, I am going to set the two of you over there at that table by the juke box, and I will buy you both drinks for as long as you will both sit there. Dexter, if you don't mind, I'll buy you drinks all night too if you want to sit with them."

"That would be a perfect end to this day." Even Dexter wasn't sure if he was being ironic or not. Besides, if Dexter were going to get any information about Don Birch and his family at the bar, Pat and Teddy would be a better source than most, if they were inclined to talk about Don or Jeff.

Neither Pat nor Teddy could pass up the prospect of free drinks, and Dexter's presence at the table made it easier for them too. Dexter was a little uneasy at first. But Dexter's beers were already taking hold. Dexter reflected on what all Sam had said about Teddy and Pat and their friendship. He envied them.

By the time regulars getting off work started milling in, the three were well on their way to feeling no pain and the ice was clearly broken between Teddy and Pat. A few people looked over, amused at the trio. But, mostly people ignored them except when Teddy and Pat would break into obnoxious fits of laughter over juvenile fart and sex jokes. A few of the jokes, Dexter could not help but laugh at.

Finally, Sam's waitress, Gina, came on duty. She had been told by Sam about the deal and appeared more than a little annoyed that she had to serve Pat and Teddy all night. Gina had a long, thick mop of purple hair growing from the top of her head. The sides of her head were close-cropped and pink. Her left ear was studded from the top to the lobe. Dexter often wondered what she was doing in a town like this. He also wondered what she would think of him if he were ten years younger.

As Gina walked away after delivering her first round for the table, Pat leaned over to Teddy and said, "Do you think the carpet matches the drapes?" To which Teddy replied "Hell, I bet she has hardwood floors." The two laughed as though this were the funniest thing they had ever heard and were hearing it for the first time. Dexter had heard them make the same joke several times before. Dexter also knew that Gina had heard it at least this time by the way she slammed her serving tray onto the bar, ten feet away.

By 10:30, Dexter's head was swimming and Pat and Teddy were professing their love for each other with tear streaked cheeks in what seemed like an apology competition.

Dexter knew he was no longer needed. He was starting to feel like a third wheel. He had also given up on trying to bring up Don Birch, so he said goodnight and headed for the door, stopping at the bar to give Gina the residue of his traveling money from his vacation as a tip. It was about $52, but probably still not enough for putting up with Teddy and Pat.

As his head hit the pillow at home Dexter realized it was just Thursday. He would not be in the office bright and early the next morning.

4

Dexter woke up to a banging on his door. He looked at his clock to realize he had overslept. It was a few minutes before noon and he was suddenly aware of a banging in his head that was keeping rhythm with the banging on his door. He opened the door to face an irritated Wilbur Pedersen. "Why weren't you in Court this morning?"

"I didn't know I had Court this morning."

"You got noticed last week."

"I was on vacation last week."

"And you've been back for two days now."

"So, what did I miss?"

"Jeremy Wilson. He violated probation twenty minutes after that last hearing right before you left on vacation. You got appointed again, we had an arraignment this morning at 10:30. The Judge rescheduled it for 1:30.

"I brought the paper work over. It was still in your District Court box. I also brought you your copy of Roy Musgrave's autopsy. Miller's and Hays' will be here next week."

"Thanks. Sorry I dropped the ball this morning on Wilson. I'll see you at 1:30."

"See you then."

Dexter was starting to wish he had not come back from vacation. He took a quick shower, shaved and dressed for Court. He took the stuff Wilbur had brought him down to the office. He held the envelope with the autopsy report, dreading the idea that he may have to look at it one day, and threw it on top of Don Birch's file. He grabbed Jeremy Wilson's last file which was still on the corner of the desk where Dexter had dropped it right before going off on his vacation.

Dexter then picked the mail up off the floor by the slot and went through it. There was nothing of interest, so he threw it on the desk and then checked his messages. The newest ones were from the Court and Wilbur Pedersen from that morning. The oldest one was from the night before, from his mother. He had not called her since he had gotten home. He called her back, got her machine and told her all was fine, and he would call at the usual time on Sunday.

Dexter looked at the clock. It was 12:45. He wanted to eat but there was no time to go to the restaurant. He lit a cigarette and grabbed a handful of quarters from a bowl on his desk and headed for the Courthouse. He stopped just inside the main entrance at the vending machines. He got two Diet Cokes, a Snicker and two bags of peanuts. He found a chair and dug into his lunch while reading Jeremy Wilson's probation violation reports.

It was unbelievable. Wilson had had a better time on Dexter's vacation than Dexter had. At least for the first week. Dexter would never understand people like Jeremy. There were all kinds of psychological explanations, including things called "personality disorders." Dexter had seen plenty of clients with the diagnosis, including Jeremy. Dexter had read up on personality disorders on his own. He had argued for leniency for clients, including Jeremy, at sentencing hearings, citing their personality disorders, schizoaffective disorders, and their addictions. But, it still frustrated Dexter. More than once, quite often actually, Dexter Smith wanted to grab his clients and shake them and tell them "Go home, eat dinner and go to bed early. Get up in the morning, early. Shower and shave and put on a shirt with a collar and go get a haircut. Then, go get a job. And, when you have that job, go to it every day and do it right and have insurance and a retirement plan. If you go to a bar and drink, walk home. If your tail light breaks, fix it. Don't do drugs. Twenty years will come and go before you know it and you will be happy."

41

Dexter would never say this. His own job and security depended on people like this. And, most, if not all his clients could kick his ass. And, deep, deep down, Dexter knew he didn't believe it himself. Dexter had drunk and smoked pot in high school and college. He had sold some of his extra pot to friends on occasion, and he had driven drunk. Hell, he even burglarized a high school once to steal some computers with a couple of college buddies.

The real difference between Dexter and some of his clients was that he never got caught. And, when he did settle down a little, he had enough brains to finish college and law school and then he found a place where he would never have to work very hard. How could he tell someone to go work in a factory or slaughter house for twenty years and be happy? What about Don Birch? He had gone to work, worked every day, built something for himself and his family. How was that turning out for Don now?

Dexter decided that no one can help who they are or will be, then he wondered what the point was. Then, he decided he was overthinking everything which was doing his hangover and his client no good. So, he downed the Snicker in two bites, having already eaten the peanuts, chugged the second Diet Coke, burped louder than he had intended to in the echoing halls of the courthouse and went over to the jail to see Jeremy before court. Jeremy wasn't in jail. Dexter had assumed he would not be able to bond out, but he had. So, Dexter went upstairs to wait for Jeremy.

Jeremy showed up ten minutes before court, wearing a Burger Hut uniform and looking very annoyed with Dexter. "Where the fuck were you? I had to take off work this morning and then again this afternoon. I'm just glad the Judge let me go back and work the lunch shift. I've only had this job for four days."

Dexter felt bad, but not bad enough to put up with Jeremy. "Look, I'm sorry. I really am. I just got back from vacation and didn't even know about the violation, much less that I was appointed to you. You just got put back on probation for Christ-sake."

Jeremy shed his anger to show the guilt and fear beneath it. "Well what are we gonna do? I got a job at Burger Hut, plus I'm doing some roof work and I hit three AA meetings this week. I've checked in and pissed clean at probation since I got out of jail."

"Why didn't you do all that two weeks ago when we walked out of here? If you had, neither of us would be here now."

"I know, I fucked-up. I'm sorry. I know you did a lot for me and I let you down."

"You didn't let me down, I get paid to do this and I will keep going home to my own bed every night that you are in prison."

"Am I going to prison this time?" Jeremy had his hands in his pockets now and was staring down at the floor.

"I hope not, but I'd be lying if I told you no. Look, we can't prove you didn't violate probation again. So, let's go in and admit this violation, ask for an update to the sentencing report to give you a few weeks to keep doing what you are doing now. It can't hurt. So, how is work at Burger Hut?"

"It sucks, but not too bad. Except for these two idiots I have to work with. I'm sorry man but these guys are total fucktards. And they are training me. They both know their shit, but it isn't that complicated. Worst part of it is, they don't get along so the boss schedules them on different days, so every day I get stuck with one or the other."

"Pat and Teddy?" Dexter didn't have to ask this. He knew it was Pat and Teddy. He hid his irritation at Jeremy for calling them "fucktards."

"I guess that's their names. I just call them the 'Middle-aged Mutant Ninja Turtles.' All either one of them can talk about is kung-foo shit. The skinny one is Teddy, right? He came in today hung-over as shit and I had to work the grill with him all through lunch and he just kept letting one nasty beer fart after another. I swear to God, I thought I was gonna puke."

Dexter fought back his smile. He realized how embarrassed he would be if Jeremy knew how much Teddy and Pat had to do with Dexter missing court earlier in the day. Would anyone want to have a lawyer who was drinking buddies with the Middle-aged Mutant Ninja Turtles?

They were in and out of Court in less than ten minutes. Dexter apologized for his absence earlier and Jeremy admitted his probation violation. Wilbur Pedersen wanted to go right to sentencing, arguing that the latest sentencing report was only a couple of weeks old and that the Judge had already told Jeremy that he had gotten his last chance at probation.

Dexter asked for an update to the last report pointing out what Jeremy had done in the last week and how little would have to be done because of the newness of the last report. He also mentioned that by working at Burger Hut along with roofing, Jeremy could pay a chunk of the restitution still owed by the next sentencing if he did go to prison. Judge Ostergart looked doubtful but agreed to the update and set a sentencing hearing.

Dexter went out of the courtroom to check his boxes in the two courts and made sure he didn't have any more hearings that day. He did find that he had gotten two new cases in county court. He took the paperwork from the new cases and went back to the office.

Back at the office, Dexter stared down at the envelope Wilbur Pedersen had given him with the autopsy report. Dexter knew there would be pictures. Dexter did not want to open that envelope today. He did not want to open it ever if it could be helped. Dexter had never wished anyone dead, especially not a nice guy like Don Birch. But, Don Birch was already dying, so Dexter wished he would be expeditious about it.

Dexter looked at the new court appointments. He had a juvenile case, In The Interest of June Grace Parker, A Minor Child. Dexter would be representing the mother, Grace June Parker. The other was a felony case, Failure to Register as a Sex Offender. Both were set for hearings on the following Wednesday.

Dexter added these to the calendar on his desk and saw that he had two simple divorce cases set for final hearing the following week too. This would be a nice week for easy money. There was nothing to fight over in the divorces; he would go into court and get the Judge's ruling, then collect on the balances still due.

Dexter opened files for the two new cases and quickly cranked out letters to the new clients introducing himself. If he got the letters in the mail before 3:30, they should have the letters by Monday.

5

Dexter spent the weekend in his apartment, recovering from his vacation and the night at the bar. Monday morning, he was in his office at 8:30, ready to go. He found two messages on his answering machine. Friday's mail must have gotten sorted and gone right out on Saturday, because the messages were from each of the two new clients. Dexter called them back and set up the appointments for later that day. The sex offender at 11:30 and Gracie June at 1:30.

The sex offender, about 22, came in with his mother. She had been the one to call and leave the message and she tried to do most of the talking at the appointment, which always annoyed Dexter. "Ma'am, I hate to interrupt you here, but I really need to. Your son is an adult, and this is his case. I am HIS lawyer. He is going to have to go in front of the Judge. He really needs to talk to me and get used to talking for himself."

The mother, a pock-marked stick of a woman with sunken jowls and eyes, and stringy straw-colored hair rolled her eyes and crossed one leg over the other. "Go ahead then, tell him," she said to the fat, rutty kid. His wiry brown curls stuck out of a ballcap pulled tight on his head. The boy looked up for the first time and started to speak, but still avoided eye contact. "Well, that girl, her cousin keeps telling me that she says she's going to tell the Judge that I didn't know she was fourteen."

Mother could not hold back any longer and cut in again "Plus, I know for a fact she screwed half the football team at her high school and she jacked off her own cousin. Her own cousin. And she's already covered in a bunch of trashy tattoos."

Dexter assumed she made it a point to say "trashy tattoos" to distinguish them from her own, classy artworks. In her spaghetti string top, cut-offs and flip flops, Dexter counted no fewer than six tattoos without trying. They appeared to all be inspired by the murals found on panel vans of the 1970s, all winged horses and wizards.

"I understand how you feel," Dexter cut in. "But I have to stop you right there. This really isn't about the other case anymore. Unless that other case is appealed, and your conviction is overturned, you are a sex offender required to register under the law. Even if it were to be overturned in the future, that would not change the fact that right now you are required to register. It will never be a defense here, for this case. This is a simple matter of did you or didn't you follow the registration requirements.

"Now, reading the affidavit for the arrest warrant, they say that you went in and registered five months ago when you moved back in with your mother. Then, you went in last month and registered your new job. But, your birthday was two months ago, and you didn't go in and register in the month of your birthday. Did you go in during the month of your birthday and register?"

"Well, no. I forgot. But I had just gone in right before and I went in last month. It's not like I'm trying to not register. They are just fuckin with me, and it's not fair."

"I agree. It's not fair. And they are fucking with you, because they can. I'm just going to be honest with you. No one cares. You are a sex offender. Does that mean you're a bad guy? No, it means when you were nineteen you made a mistake with a fourteen-year-old girl. But, cops enforce the law and maybe they don't like you, for whatever reason." Looking at the mother and son, Dexter could imagine that more than one cop knew the family and didn't care too much for them. "So, they use this law as a reason to arrest you. And the law is pretty clear.

"Is it right? No. Will it change? No. Why? Because politicians make laws and only politicians change laws. No state senator is going to stand up in the legislature and say, 'I want to make the sex offender registry laws fairer to sex offenders.' It would be political suicide. Most people out there don't understand, and they aren't going to take the time to see the sex offenders' side of things. The average person, who doesn't really have anything to do with any of this thinks that if you have to register, you are a dangerous pervert and always will be. They think 'sex offender' they think 'child molester.' It's not right and I'm sorry. There is nothing I can do."

Dexter had given this speech many times. It was an easy sales pitch because it was true. And, here came the hook.

"But, Judge Ostergart understands, and he doesn't like the law as it is. And, Mr. Pedersen, the county attorney, he understands too. So, if we waive the preliminary hearing in county court on Wednesday, the case will go to District Court, and they will let you plead to a misdemeanor, attempted failure to register charge, and you will get a two hundred dollar fine from the Judge. You are done. But, you only get this deal once. So, don't make this mistake again." They weren't thrilled with what he had to say, but they understood and were ok with it. Mom had never gotten over her surliness, but by the time she left, Dexter was pretty sure it wasn't directed at him.

Dexter followed the mother and son out of his office on his way to lunch. Dexter watched them climb into a dilapidated Chevy pick-up, grind it into reverse, and back-out into the street. There was something written in white paint on one of the tires. It took a second or two to register with Dexter what it said. Then, he made it out. "No Hunting."

After lunch at Lee Ho Fook's, Dexter settled back into his chair and started to review the Parker file. Dexter would represent Gracie June, Tom McWilliams would be the Guardian Ad Litem for the baby, and John Miller would be the attorney for the as yet to be determined father.

Grace June Parker's daughter, June Grace Parker, was three weeks old, and had been born with a cleft lip that would require surgery in the first three to six months after birth. The child was healthy otherwise, but the cleft lip required special feeding instructions. Mother had agreed to voluntary services with HHS at the insistence of mother's brother, Wendel Parker, to help mother learn to properly feed and care for the baby. Uncle was capable and willing to care for the child, including feeding, bathing and changing diapers. Concerns reported to the Department by mother included her own inability to wake up at night to feed the child when the child cried out and mother's concerns about her own ability to care for the child when her brother, child's uncle, was at work. Last doctor visit, child had not gained weight. Department intervened after consulting with the county attorney. Child remains in home with mother and uncle for time being, with intensive in-home services.

Dexter put the report down and let out a sigh. There were two things that surprised Dexter in this report, Harley was willing, interested and capable of caring for this child; and Harley had a job.

About this time, Gracie June walked in with a man behind her. It was Harley, but he was wearing a shirt with a collar that was tucked into a pair of blue Dickies and a belt. And, Harley was clean shaven, and his hair was cut. His hair was clean. Harley was clean. Gracie June was clean.

"Hello Grace, hello Harley. Have a seat."

"It's ok, you can call me Wendel. Is it ok if I stay?"

"Sure, if it's ok with your sister, I think it would be a very good idea. Is it ok with you Grace?"

"Yeah, I think it's a good idea too, Wendel's been a big help to me with June Grace. The way he acts, you would think he was the father."

She surely didn't intend for that to sound the way it did. Dexter and Wendel both winced a little when she said it. Each knew what the other was thinking but wanted to move on. So, Dexter changed the subject.

"So, you named the baby after yourself."

"No, I named her after my mother, June, and my grandmother, Grace."

"But, you are too, aren't you?"

"No, I'm named after my grandmother, Grace, and my mother, June."

And with that, Dexter had completely forgotten about Gracie June's comment about Wendel being the father of her child.

"Look, Mr. Smith. You have to help us. I mean, help Gracie. I, we just love that little June bug, and we can't lose her. It has been just the two of us for so long. It is nice to have other family again."

Wendel first described to Dexter how he had gotten a job at the packing plant and how, once June Grace was six weeks old, he could take her to daycare. Wendel was convinced that even if his sister couldn't care for her child, he could. When he finished talking, he had convinced Dexter as well. All Dexter had to do was get them through the next three weeks, until she could go to daycare, without the baby being pulled from the home.

"The arraignment is in two days. We need to know what the state has in mind. If you admit, the Department will be in your life for a long time. If we deny, they could try to pull the baby out of the home and set the adjudication right away. I have to talk with the case worker and the county attorney. We also need to know where Tom McWilliams stands on all of this. He is the GAL and we will need him on our side."

What Dexter said was a little technical and sometimes needed explaining to clients not used to the system. While Wendel and Grace were far from sophisticated, they were no strangers to the system. They understood Dexter all too well.

After Wendel and Gracie June left the office, Dexter decided he needed a break, so he grabbed some quarters from the bowl on his desk and headed over to the courthouse for a Snicker and Diet Coke. He would check his boxes in both courts and pop in to see Wilbur Pedersen. In other words, he was going to generally fart around, but in a way that made him feel productive.

After woofing down the Snicker and Diet Coke, Dexter checked his box in each court and headed down the hall to the back of the courthouse and the County Attorney's office.

Dexter was met by the County Attorney's staff with their usual indifference. The front office was cramped for the three ladies working there, behind the counter that separated them from anyone who happened through the door. The counter, doors, trim and floor were all original wood, stained and worn with age. The walls were white and lined with filing cabinets, some were wood, matching the floor and trim, others were metal. They were a mix match of sizes and colors, added from time to time over the years as they were needed. They marked time in the county attorney's office, eras in the county's history like layers of dirt marking eras in geologic time.

Dexter made his way to Wilbur's corner office and stood at the open door until he was acknowledged and told to come in. Dexter informed Wilbur of the two meetings he had had that day with his two new clients. Wilbur agreed on the plan for the sex offender. But he interrupted Dexter halfway through his plan for Gracie June. "What are you talking about? Whose Wendel? You mean Harley Parker?"

"Look Wilbur, this guy has really done a one eighty, haircut, shower, shave, job. He even changed his name back to Wendel. He has really turned it around and he has a good plan."

"Forget it. You aren't going to win that one Dexter. It isn't going to happen, and you should have never let those people think that it could.

"That poor kid. No telling who her father is, and that cleft lip. She is darker than most people around here if you haven't noticed. And, I know it's not right, but kids will be cruel about stuff like that, and the lip. She would have it bad enough around here without leaving her in a home with that bunch. No!"

Wilbur leaned back and took a package off the credenza behind his desk.

"Here, we got the other autopsy reports. You need to focus your attention on this case anyway."

"Why? I'm just going to file continuances until my client dies."

"Well, it may not be going away that easy after all. Rumor has it your client and his wife went to the doctor on Friday, his electronic monitor confirms that, and scuttlebutt is your client walked out of that office happy as a clam. Like he had a new lease on life. And, half the staff out at the clinic then heard Dr. Jones on the phone with some oncology resident in Omaha, reading him the riot act and threatening to report him to the medical board in Lincoln."

Dexter's heart sank. He didn't want to believe what he had just heard. And, he did not want to have to open the package he was just given, or the other package sitting back in his office. "Oh, come on Will. You know how people like to talk in this town. I wouldn't believe a word of it."

"I don't believe it. I don't disbelieve it. I am going to prepare for all possibilities. I would advise you to do the same. Don't let this catch you with your pants down."

Dexter left the courthouse, irritated with Wilbur Pedersen. Dexter decided to make his way down to Tom McWilliam's office to try and lobby Tom for support in the Grace June/June Grace case.

"I don't know Dex. That kid is going to have it tough. She is going to need a lot of care. I went out the other day with the case worker. I agree they are trying. But, for Christ's sake. They have an interior door on the outside of their trailer and about a quarter of the windows are broken out with just plastic over them. They are going to have to get all that fixed before winter. I just don't know."

"Look Tom, you have to give reunification a chance. That's just the law. And, if it's so bad now, why haven't they removed the baby?

"As soon as she is six weeks old, Wendel can take her to daycare while he is at work. Once she is big enough for the surgery, the feeding won't be such a problem for Grace. I'm going to have her deny. Just give us a few weeks. We don't even need the adjudication hearing. Let's just set it for pre-adjudication hearing in a few weeks and see how things are then. Family support can stay in this thing for that long, so the baby will be fine."

"You aren't asking for much, I guess. It just seems that way because of who we're dealing with. I will go along with it, for now. And, I'll let Wilbur know where I stand on all of this and he will back down too.

"But, have Harley get that door and those windows taken care of.

"Why are you so gung-ho about this case? Don't you have a triple murder trial to get ready for?"

"Yeah, I am really wishing they had given that to you, or John."

"John is a victim's cousin. And I'm up to my ass in another victim's estate."

"Well, I hate to admit it, but I'm going to be relieved when my client kicks the bucket himself."

"Word is, that may not be happening as soon as he thought. Won't that be a pisser?" Christ, Dexter just couldn't get away from this. He knew shooting the messenger was senseless, but Dexter found himself growing as irritated with Tom has he had been with Wilbur just a few minutes earlier.

"I haven't heard much about it except for some rumors, and I am sure they are just that. I will see you later Tom." Dexter fled back to his office and checked his phone messages. He didn't have any. It was 3:45, close enough to call it a day. He locked the office door and went upstairs until dinner, trying futilely to push out of his head the possibility that his client wasn't dying; and Dexter was going to have to defend someone on three counts of murder.

The hearing for Grace June went as Dexter and Tom had planned. There was a pre-adjudication hearing set for the following month. There was a team meeting set up as well that would include, Grace, Wendel, the case workers and all the attorneys in the case. That was where the case would really be won or lost.

The sex offender waived his preliminary hearing and was given a District Court arraignment date. The divorces Dexter had to finish up went off without a hitch and Dexter collected his fees for them. It was a day more productive for Dexter than most weeks.

6

The next few weeks were pretty uneventful in the life and law practice of Dexter Smith. He wasn't getting many cases and didn't know if it was due to a downtick in crime or if Judge Anderson was just reducing Dexter's number of appointments due to the murder case.

Dexter still hadn't looked at the autopsy reports. He hadn't looked at the police reports since the day of the preliminary hearing and he hadn't heard from his client.

The week remained slow until Thursday, when the phone rang. It was Don Birch's wife. The District Court arraignment was coming up, so she made an appointment for her husband the next afternoon.

Dexter thought this was a perfect way to end the week. He would meet with Don, find out when he would be dying, then close the office early and start the weekend.

Don Birch looked much more his old self as he walked into Dexter's office the next afternoon. He wore his trademark gingham work shirt and Rustlers with western belt and pointy toed boots. His wife was a thin, stern woman in a double-knit pant suit and had one of those tall hair-dos like Marge had on The Simpsons, only not as tall, or blue. She carried a white patent leather purse in the crook of her arm close to her, like it contained the crown jewels, or all her family's skeletons. Dexter had encountered the woman only a few times in the years he had been in town, but quickly remembered she was a fussy, disapproving woman. She seemed quite the opposite of her husband.

Dexter welcomed them in, offering them seats. Dexter noticed that Don was not quite his old self as he had appeared at first. Don was quiet and reserved. Don smiled but avoided eye contact.

"You look well Don. How are you doing?"

"Well, Mr. Smith, uh, Dexter. I uh, well I guess I am doing a lot better than we first thought. I guess my pancreatic cancer isn't cancer after all."

Don and his wife looked at each other and smiled, both tried but failed to make it a smile of relief that Don wasn't dying. The smiles trailed of, they both looked down at the floor and her right hand and his left, which had been clinched together, suddenly released and fell to their sides.

"Well Don. That's. That's very good news." Dexter knew how lame he sounded, but what the hell else was he going to say? The natural thing to say would be something like "Well, shit, you stupid bastard, why the hell did you go and kill off all your in-laws then? What the hell do you expect me to do for you now?" Nope, he couldn't say that, as reasonable as it would have been under the circumstances.

"So, what was the mix-up?"

"Well, I told you about my stomach problems. Turns out, I have early onset diabetes and some kind of stones in my pancreas. Islet cell tumors are what they are called. They can be cancer, but mine aren't. Dr. Jones said the young doctor in Omaha who read my tests should have asked for more tests before he made the diagnosis."

"He never should have called you." Mrs. Birch cut in. "So now, Mr. Smith, I have a husband who is very sick, but with a very treatable condition and three daughters who have been made widows much too soon." Don's eyes shot daggers into his wife when she said this, but he instantly composed himself and looked back down at the floor, nodding his head in agreement.

"Mr. Smith, my husband tells me that you mentioned another lawyer you would recommend in a case like this."

This insulted Dexter a little, that suddenly he may not be good enough to handle the case, but right away he remembered that he didn't think he was a good enough lawyer for this case and that he didn't even want this case.

But, he did not remember suggesting anyone and his expression showed that.

Don Birch quickly grasped Dexter's memory loss and piped in "You remember, that day in the jail, you talked about how you weren't this guy, and then started talking about Perry Mason. His name was Darryl, or something like that."

Dexter laughed, then caught himself. "Darrow, Clarence Darrow. I'm pretty sure he doesn't practice anymore."

The look on Mrs. Birch's face told Dexter that she knew who Clarence Darrow was, even if her husband did not. So, she and Dexter quickly brought Don up to speed on famous criminal cases of the late nineteenth and early twentieth centuries.

"Frankly Mr. Smith, I know you are a fine public defender. But, you have never had a case like my husband's, have you? Besides, we are not indigent. I don't understand how he qualifies for your services. We are not poor people."

Dexter saw right through this. This was about Mrs. Birch's pride. She had been making excuses all her married life for this man and no matter how well he had provided for his family, no matter what he had built up, he was never going to be good enough. Having a public defender instead of a "lawyer" just proved that to her.

"Mrs. Birch, almost anyone in this county would qualify for a public defender in a case like this. This is not your average case. A murder trial takes about a year to prepare for, several hundred billable hours just for the lawyers. On top of that you are billed for support staff, you will have to take depositions of all the witnesses. Those depositions can be a few thousand dollars. Then you have to hire experts to counter their experts and they can cost more per hour than the lawyers. Then you have to take depositions of the experts and pay the experts for their time being deposed.

"Conservatively, you are talking fifty thousand dollars. And that is being very conservative. Then you have to consider there is only one other attorney in this town who would take a case like this, and he is conflicted out of it because he represents your late son-in-law's estate. A small firm or solo practitioner would need to be paid most of the money upfront because this case would take up so much time, they won't have time to take any more work. A case like this would kill their revenue stream.

"Big firms from Omaha or Lincoln would charge twice as much per hour and bill you for mileage and driving time out here. They would basically cost you a hundred and fifty thousand dollars. Your best bet would be a North Platte or Grand Island firm. And, they would still cost quite a bit."

The Birches sat and let this sink in. "What about Kearney?" Mrs. Birch asked.

"There are some good lawyers in Kearney. But, you have to be careful, there are lawyers in every town who would drag this case out twice as long as it needs to be, do unnecessary work to run up a bill they would know you can't pay, irritate the judge, the prosecutor and a jury and make this much, much worse than it already is. There are some pretty exceptional lawyers down in Dawson County, but I don't know if any of them would take this case right now.

"This I why I say most people would qualify for a public defender in a case like this. There is also the Commission on Public Advocacy. They are a state agency who are mostly known for doing appeals for people on death row. But, they also come out-state to smaller communities like ours to help in cases like this. I could easily get the Judge to appoint them to help me. And, if I am not up to this task, they can take over."

"You are up to it." Don Birch sat up firm in his chair. He had let his wife do the talking up till now, but he had made up his mind. He looked Dexter in the eye "Dexter, you have just explained a lot to us we didn't know. My wife's a lot smarter than me, and I don't think she had any idea what we were looking at here. You just explained it how both of us can understand. Plus, I like you and I may be wrong, but I think that matters as much as anything. Besides, you have those commission fellows to help if you do get stuck."

With that, the covenant was sealed. Dexter knew Don had faith in him. And that gave Dexter faith in himself. Dexter Smith had an opportunity to be the kind of lawyer he had not even imagined being in a very, very long time.

"So, do you really think this could take a year?" Don asked, sounding a bit overwhelmed.

"It very well could. A murder trial with just one victim could take that long. This will almost be like three murder trials."

"Will they do that?" Mrs. Birch wanted to know. "Will there be three separate trials?"

"I don't think so. That's called bifurcation. I don't think we would want that, it would give them three separate chances to convict. And they only need one conviction to get Don life without parole. I can't imagine right now why they would want it. The prosecution rarely wants to bifurcate."

So, Dexter and the Birches spent the rest of the meeting going over various fine points of procedure that were relevant to the arraignment and what their first steps would be in discovery for the case. It didn't take long. Dexter would have to get started right away reviewing what he had so far, being all the police reports from every deputy or state trooper who had written one and, Dexter would have to read the autopsy reports, and look at the pictures. Dexter now knew how he would be spending his weekend.

After eating dinner with the family at the Chinese restaurant, Dexter walked down to The Pawnee Club. He took his Busch Light to the back door of the bar to have a cigarette. Teddy and Pat were out back talking to the dishwasher who was on break. Dexter exchanged pleasantries, finished his smoke and his beer and headed back into the bar for his second beer and to visit with Sam Hagan.

"Well Sam, looks like I'm in for it."

"What's that Dex?"

"Don Birch isn't dying after all"

"Oh, yeah, I heard about that. Everyone's been talking about that. You really need to get down here more. I heard those funerals were really something. Of course, the killings are old news now. Everyone is now talking about how Don's youngest daughter, Linda Hays, is already practically engaged."

"No shit? I have to start cracking on that case this weekend and get up to speed. I'm going to have to figure all this family dynamic shit out too. And I don't quite know how to go about asking my client and his wife about that. Probably wouldn't get an accurate answer anyway."

Sam provided as much as he knew about the family, including all the rumors that circulated after the killings and then the funerals. What everyone agreed on was that Roy Musgrave was a complete asshole, if a rich one, who wanted to get rid of his crippled wife. And, Scott Miller was a drunk who beat on his wife and would probably kill her one day. But, no one knew why Don would kill Jeff Hays. It was like Don was just killing to be killing at that point. Complete the pattern of killing sons-in-law.

"That's what confuses everyone Dexter, why Jeff? He was a damn good kid. He was a lot like Don. The other two were nothing like Don. And, now, his wife has already taken up with that old flame of hers, Will Jorgensen." Sam just shook his head and wiped down the spot on the bar in front of Dexter. "Time was Dexter, you would have thought Jeff was Don's son, instead of his son-in-law." Sam just kept wiping and shaking his head.

Dexter mulled this over a bit. He had worried about talking to the daughters. He knew he would probably have to at some point, even if it was just to depose them. Now, with one not acting at all like a grieving widow, Dexter wondered if he could talk to Linda Hays. Maybe she would be willing to shed light on what everyone else was wondering: Why did Don kill Jeff if Jeff was such a nice guy?

Next, Dexter asked who Will Jorgensen was. Sam explained that Will had grown up in the area and had been a high school sweetheart of Linda Hays. His family had owned Jorgensen Realty in town for three generations, but when Will's father died, Will's mother sold the business and moved off with the kids. The current owners of Jorgensen Realty, who had bought the place from Will's mother, kept the name for goodwill. Then, about a year ago, Will Jorgensen showed back up in town wanting to work in the old family firm. The new owners thought it wouldn't hurt business to have a Jorgensen working for Jorgensen Realty, so they hired him on. Some around town were thinking that Will and Linda had rekindled their old flame before Jeff was killed.

"Dexter, you would know most of this already if you came in here more. It hurts my feelings I haven't seen much of you lately."

"Yeah, well, the last time I was here I got pretty hammered with a couple of kung-foo fry cooks. I took that as a sign that maybe I should cut back on social activities for a while."

Sam just laughed at this and moved down the bar to refill drinks. When he finally made his way back to Dexter, Sam looked more serious. "So, I know you can't really talk about it, but what are you going to do? Do you think you can get him out of this?"

"Hell, I don't see how anyone can. I just don't want to embarrass myself. And, if Don Birch spends the rest of his life in prison I don't want him or anyone else saying it was because he got stuck with some sorry, hick lawyer who didn't know shit from apple butter. So, I better finish this beer and get to it. Some way to spend a weekend."

61

"Well, if you're going to try acclimating to work at your age, you're going to need plenty of breaks and lots of moral support. So, don't be a stranger."

"You may be right but, promise me you won't let me get stupid drunk until this case is over. I suddenly have a reputation to consider."

"Deal."

Dexter went home, lit a cigarette, flopped on the couch and began reading police reports. He paced himself all weekend, taking lots of breaks to nap, eat and even watch a couple of movies. But all in all, he had made real progress and had taken lots to notes. He had finally broken down and looked at the autopsies. The reports were all very clinical and even boring for the most part. As the pathologist would have put it "unremarkable." Even the photos were not as bad as he thought they would be. While not at all pleasant, on the slabs in the clean, clinical settings, the bodies weren't much more unpleasant to look at than roadkill. Still, Dexter had made it a point to review the autopsies and photos at three o'clock Saturday afternoon in hopes that any horror from looking at them would wear off before bedtime.

It was all looking open and closed for the prosecution. What cocky lawyers like to call "a slam dunk." It bothered Dexter, it wouldn't matter who the defense lawyer was. It was looking like Don had no defense. Still, Dexter worried about his reputation. If John Miller or Tom McWilliams had the case and lost it, it would be assumed the case was unwinnable. Dexter had something to prove, if only to himself. He at least wanted to go down swinging, draw a little blood off Wilbur Pedersen. Wilbur was going to win, but he could sweat a little to get the win. For perhaps the first time in his career, Dexter truly cared about what people would think of him. He wanted some respect.

By 8:30 Sunday evening, he had reviewed everything but the video of Don's confession to Bob Anderson. He went down to the office with the DVD and put it in his desktop. Chief Deputy Bob Anderson was ready to interview Don Birch, but first, Bob read Don his Miranda rights and then he had Don read the Miranda waiver and sign it. Then, Bob said "Now Don, tell it all to me again, just like you told it to me in the car on the way over here." Dexter could not believe his ears.

Was it going to really be that easy? Had Bob Anderson, of all people, screwed-up? Up until now, Dexter had found some minor discrepancies in times. Jeff Hays' neighbor reported hearing gunshots at almost the same time Don Birch was seen leaving the car dealership. It was probably a mistake on someone's part, but it could raise some kind of reasonable doubt.

But now, there was possibly a suppressible issue, the confession. Dexter went back up to his apartment and looked through all the reports written by deputies who had had any contact with Don when he was first confronted and taken into custody, including Bob Anderson. Sure enough, none had read Don his rights before Bob had taken him into the station. It could just be nothing, but this would explain why Bob Anderson had been so nervous at the preliminary hearing, and why Wilbur had seemed so irritated with Bob. Dexter had an argument to make now. There was still enough circumstantial evidence and an eyewitness that put Don at one of the murders. And, if Don took the stand, a suppressed confession could still be used to rebut any of his testimony. But, Dexter now had something to go down swinging with. But, in doing so, he was going to piss-off and embarrass the toughest and most respected cop in the county. Dexter's new-found respect would come at a price.

7

First thing Monday morning, Dexter called Don Birch to confirm that he was placed in cuffs and put in the back of Bob Anderson's patrol vehicle on the night of the murders and confessed everything to Bob on the way to the station without having been Mirandized.

"I know what my rights are, I've heard them a million times on tv."

"But, are you sure you didn't hear them from Bob until you got to the sheriff's office?"

"Yeah, because when we were walking into the station from the car, he asked me about it. I think he thought that young deputy who put the cuffs on me told them to me then. He got kind of nervous and a little irritated at that point."

"So, did Bob ask you questions in the patrol unit or did you just blurt out what had happened?"

"No, he asked me what was going on; if I had anything to do with the killings. So, I started telling him, and he kept asking 'Well, then what happened?'"

Dexter went on to explain the importance of all of this to Don, and then had to repeat it all to Don's wife when Don put her on the phone. They wanted to know what it all meant and how it would affect the case. This frustrated Dexter because he really wasn't sure yet. It would certainly make it hard to prosecute all three murders if the confession was suppressed. Maybe Don would only be looking at one or two life sentences instead of three. The real victory would be that Dexter could do something. He wouldn't look like a hapless hick lawyer after all. Hell, maybe he could plead this thing down to a manslaughter, just so the prosecutor and sheriff's office wouldn't be too embarrassed at a public trial.

When the arraignment rolled around, Dexter walked into District Court in a nice newish gray pinstripe suit he had picked-up at a Salvation Army in Lincoln the last time he had been there. Widows of rich men always sent their late husbands' suits to the Salvation Army or Goodwill. Dexter had gotten more than a few five hundred-dollar suits for twenty bucks in his life. It was the first reason he had had to wear the suit, so anyone who noticed it thought he had gone all out and bought a new suit for the big case. He was also carrying the briefcase he rarely used. In it was the motion to suppress he had drafted the day before.

As he entered the courtroom, scanning the room for his client, the first person Dexter noticed was Charlie Pedersen. Charles Wilbur Pedersen, III was a third-year law student and the son of County Attorney C. Wilbur Pedersen. Charlie was a handsome, affable you man, dressed in khakis and a golf shirt. Dexter had known plenty of guys like Charlie in law school and had been intimidated by them. But, Dexter liked Charlie. Charlie had always been easy for Dexter to get along with. Dexter didn't know if it was because Dexter was older and now practicing law, or if it was because Charlie was genuinely more likable than those guys in law school.

"Hey Dex. Are you going to give my old man a run for his money on this one?"

"I doubt it Charlie. Especially if he has you clerking for him on the case."

"Oh, no. I'm clerking at an immigration non-profit in Omaha right now. I just came out for the week and thought I would watch the show."

Dexter didn't say it, but he was a little surprised to hear Charlie was clerking at an immigration clinic. Dexter wondered what the unsinkable Mildred Pedersen thought of her grandson doing such a thing.

Soon, Don Birch and Dexter were seated at the defense table. Everyone was in their places and the bailiff cried out

"Please Rise." Everyone stood as Judge Ostergart entered and took his seat before telling everyone one else to be seated. The room was filled with mostly the same crowd that had filled the County Courtroom for the preliminary hearing before.

The Judge asked Don if he were Donald Alan Birch, if he could read, write and speak the English language, and if he were under the influence of any alcohol, drug or other mind-altering substance. Don answered all these questions appropriately and then the Judge read him his rights. Don assured the Judge that he had heard those rights, understood them, and had no questions about them. The Judge then read the Information to Don which charged him with three counts of first degree murder, one count of use of a deadly weapon to commit a felony and one count of use of a firearm to commit a felony. Judge Ostergart then asked Dexter how his client would plead, and Dexter answered, "Not guilty."

Don affirmed that and then entered his plea of "not guilty," the Judge authorized all discovery, including the deposing of all witnesses and made it reciprocal. Then the Judge and lawyers discussed the case progression. It was agreed that the case would be set for trial in six months, but given the nature of the case, the Judge would grant liberal continuances for a reasonable time after the six months for good cause.

Then the Judge asked Wilbur if there was anything further and Wilbur said "no." The disappointed crowd figured the hearing was over without any of the excitement they had come for. Then the Judge asked Dexter the same question. A titillating charge ran through the crowd and everyone leaned forward in unison when Dexter said "Yes, Your Honor, I have prepared a motion to suppress that I would like to file at this time." Dexter took the motion out of his briefcase. He handed Wilbur his copy and after being granted permission to approach the bench, Dexter walked up and handed the Judge the original.

66

Now, walking back to the defense table, Dexter saw that all eyes were on him, except for Wilbur Pedersen, who was reading the motion, and Bob Anderson, sitting on the front row of the gallery, whose temples were visibly throbbing as he stared at the floor between his feet.

The Judge read the motion thoughtfully and turned to Wilbur. "Mr. Pedersen, did the State know about this motion?"

"We anticipated it, Your Honor. We have tentatively prepared for it."

The Judge looked at the two accordion files and the big, white three-ring binder on the prosecutor's table. "It looks like you are ready now. Can we take this matter up this afternoon?"

Wilbur shrugged, and agreed to get the matter over with that afternoon. He knew he was not going to win this no matter how much he prepared. He also knew he wouldn't need to win it to get a conviction at trial. His only real hope had been that Dexter would not catch Bob Anderson's mistake.

Dexter went back to his office. Locked the door and pulled down the shades. He lit a cigarette and inhaled deeply. His mind raced, and his hands trembled as he tried to go over the notes he had from the case law he had used to prepare the motion. He looked over the questions he had written down that he would have to ask Bob Anderson to establish his legal argument for the suppression.

It was all coming too fast. He knew other lawyers did this all the time, but he usually avoided such work when he could. Dexter had to calm down and think. He looked at his watch. It was ten in the morning.

Dexter knocked three times on the back door of The Pawnee Club and checked the knob. It was open. "Sam? Anybody home?" Dexter was looking down the narrow corridor that lead from the back door into the bar. Just ahead to the left was the cooler. To the right, a few feet ahead was the door to Sam's office from which now protruded Sam's head. As Dexter walked closer he noticed that Sam was wearing half-glasses and holding a yellow notepad.

"Dex? I know I told you not to be a stranger, but isn't this a little early in the day?"

Dexter walked into Sam's office. He was about to explain himself but was startled to see Gina, the barmaid, sitting at a computer with Quick-Books opened on it.

"Oh, hey, sorry to interrupt anything."

"It's ok Dexter. Gina's my bookkeeper as well as barmaid. What's up?"

"Well, Sam, I need a favor."

"Shoot, what is it?"

Dexter's eyes moved from Sam to Gina who was absorbed in her computer and acted like she did not know Dexter was even there. "Well, what is it Dexter?"

Dexter filled Sam in on everything that had gone on that morning in Court as well as what he had found in the reports and what the whole motion to suppress was about in general. "Sam, I can't stop shaking. I can't go to the hearing like this. I need a bracer."

Because it was Dexter Smith saying this, it took Sam a moment to realize what was being asked. Then, they both looked down the hallway to the bar and Sam broke into a laugh. "Go sit at the bar and help yourself to what you need. When we finish-up here and start getting ready to open for lunch, you can use the office."

Dexter was on his third Jack Daniels on ice when Sam came out of the office about forty-five minutes later. He had downed the first one right away, just to downshift. The second one went a little slower. He had been nursing this third one for about half an hour as he reviewed his notepad in front of him. He was calm now, if feeling a slight buzz. He knew that would be gone by the time the hearing rolled around. He had also composed himself and absorbed all he needed to get through the hearing as well as win it.

"You need the office now big fella?" Sam was standing behind the bar with his hands on his hips. He was Dexter's closest friend, and he looked worried. He had no idea what Dexter must have been feeling right then.

Dexter looked up and smiled "No, Sam, I'm good now. I am as ready as I will ever be. And I feel pretty good about it actually."

Sam was relieved. He really was a good friend to Dexter. "Dexter, I know you can do this. When it comes to your reputation as a lawyer, you are your own worst critic. I know plenty of people you've done work for who were grateful for your help. You know all this stuff, you had to learn all this once to pass your law school classes, and you had to learn it again to pass the bar exam."

Dexter was feeling even better now. He relaxed a little and started going over his game plan with Sam, especially the surprise he had just come up with.

"Wow, Dexter, I don't know anything about this stuff, but that sounds risky."

"Well, it might be, but winning this suppression hearing won't do me much good otherwise. I have to go outside of the box if I am going to do Don any good at all."

About this time, Gina strolled in from the back to grab a root beer from the cooler. She got a cigarette from the pack in her purse on the end of the bar and headed for the back door.

"So, that's your bookkeeper?"

"Yep. And she's a good one too."

"Really?"

"You know she's my niece, don't you?"

"Oh, no. I never knew that Sam."

"Well, step-niece. She is my brother-in-law's step-daughter. But he raised her, so the wife and I think of her as a niece. She went to community college and studied business management and art. We all thought she would go on to a four-year school or move to Omaha or Denver, or some place. But, she came back here and asked me for a job. Then she started doing my books and now she keeps books for everyone in the family with a business. It is just a few hours here and a few hours there. But, it adds ups. I think she does pretty well for herself."

Dexter sat back and absorbed this. It dawned on Dexter that Gina could take care of herself working no harder than he worked taking care of himself. And, she had managed to do it with far fewer years of college.

Dexter returned to Court that afternoon after a typical lunch at Lee Ho Fook's and a quick shower. He had on the same suit and tie as that morning, but had put on a fresh shirt and undies. He was ready to go to work.

Judge Ostergart rapped the Court into session and called the case up. It was the Defendant's motion to suppress the confession but the State's burden to refute it, so the State had to start the proceeding with its evidence. The Court had to review all evidence in the light most favorable to the State.

Wilbur Pedersen called Bob Anderson to the stand and the questioning went just as it had at the preliminary hearing. When Wilbur finished, it was Dexter's turn. Bob Anderson turned slightly in the witness chair to face Dexter. Bob was calm and every ounce the criminal justice professional, but Dexter could not know this, because he was too timid to look up at Bob. Dexter buried his face in his notes. Don sat next to his lawyer, looking sheepishly from the Judge, to Bob, to the notes Dexter was reviewing.

Dexter finally began his questioning. "Chief Deputy Anderson, did you read my client his Miranda rights?"

"Yes, I did."

"Did you have him sign an acknowledgement and waiver of his rights?"

"Yes, I did."

"When did you read him these rights and have him sign the waiver?"

"When I took him into the interview room at the department, just before I recorded his confession."

"Was this the first time you had heard my client's confession?"

"No. It was not. He had already given the same statement to me in my patrol car on the way to the station."

"Had he blurted this out then, or had you asked for it?"

"Maybe a little bit of both. I asked him what had happened, and he just spilled everything. He didn't need much coaxing, but I guess a couple of times I asked, 'Then what happened?'"

Dexter had gotten the opportunity since Sunday afternoon to review Bob's in-car video. What Bob said was exactly what had been said that night. Dexter knew that Bob had reviewed the tape too, to remember everything so clearly now.

"Was Donald Birch under arrest at the time he was in your car, when you were driving him to the station?"

"No, he was not."

"What was his status at that time?"

"He was being detained for questioning."

"Was he in custody?"

"I suppose so."

"Was he free to leave?"

"No, Mr. Smith, he was not."

"Chief Deputy Anderson, why did you question my client while he was in custody, in your patrol vehicle without reading him his Miranda rights?"

"I thought the deputy who detained Mr. Birch and turned him over to me had informed Mr. Birch of his rights."

"So, it was the other deputy's fault?"

"No sir. It was my fault alone. I thought to ask Mr. Birch about his rights as we were walking into the station and that is when he informed me that he had not been read his rights yet."

Bob Anderson looked at Dexter with a somewhat relaxed smile. It was friendly. What had been done was now done and they would all move on. There had not been much press at the arraignment that morning, so none of them knew to be at this hearing. Besides, Don Birch killing his three sons-in-law was old news. It would get little coverage until the actual trial. And, as far as the State was concerned, they could prosecute Don Birch and get a conviction with or without his confession.

Dexter quick-walked the Chief Deputy through his testimony to make sure he had covered everything, then informed the Court he had no more questions. The prosecution had no more witnesses and the defense rested without putting on any of its own evidence.

The Judge laced his fingers together in front of himself and screwed-up his mouth and squinted his eyes in thought. "Mr. Pedersen. I am inclined to rule right now on this matter unless the State would like time to brief the matter."

If there had been any briefing to do, Wilbur Pedersen would have already done it. Or, he would have had his current pair of deputy county attorneys brief it. Wilbur knew he had lost this one. But, it didn't matter.

"No, Your Honor, that will not be necessary."

"Well, then, I will draft a formal ruling by the end of the week, but I hereby rule that the Defendant's motion to suppress his confession is well-founded, and in the light most favorable to the State, the evidence presented today shows that it should be and hereby is GRANTED.

"Is there anything else from the State at this time, Mr. Pedersen?"

"No, Your Honor."

"Anything else from the Defense, Mr. Smith?"

"Yes, Your Honor."

For the second time that day the Courtroom bristled with Dexter's answer to this question. "Your Honor, in light of the ruling just made by this Court, I think, under the circumstances it would be appropriate to bifurcate these counts."

"Do I understand you correctly, Mr. Smith? Are you suggesting that the counts in this case be separated out into three distinct cases?"

"I object, Your Honor" cried Wilbur Pedersen in an uncharacteristic outburst of rage.

"Hold it, Mr. Pedersen. Mr. Smith, am I understanding you correctly?"

"Yes, Your Honor. The Court has heard the evidence. The only evidence linking these three homicides together is a confession that has now been suppressed. Each is alleged to have occurred in a different location and at different times, making them all distinct and separate crimes, if all three were in fact crimes. I would ask the Court to grant this motion to avoid giving the State an unfair advantage when it is clearly their burden to prove my client guilty of all of the charges."

The Judge turned, smiling to Wilbur Pedersen "Well, Mr. Pedersen. Do you have any reason as to why I should not grant that motion?"

"I certainly don't want the Court to grant that motion, Your Honor. But, I can't, at this time, make a good legal argument as to why the Court should not grant the motion."

"The Defendant's motion to bifurcate the counts into three distinct cases is granted. I will address this matter in my written order on the motion to suppress. That order will also set out dates for progression hearings in each of the cases."

Dexter was stunned. He had managed to do what he had talked to Sam about trying earlier. It had seemed like a good idea when it had come to him. It had seemed like a good idea when he had explained it to Sam. But was it? He could see the stunned look of his client from the corner of his eye. Don Birch looked from Dexter to his wife sitting behind him. Dexter had just explained to them why bifurcation was not in their interest. Now, he had to explain why it was. But, was it? Dexter looked up and made eye contact with the old Judge. The Judge smiled down at Dexter, nodding his head. Dexter turned to Wilbur Pedersen. Wilbur's jaw pulsated in thought, his eyes were cast downward on the notes on his table. Dexter realized Wilbur was staring right through the notes.

Yes, Dexter thought at last with confidence. This was exactly the right thing to do.

A few minutes later in his office, Dexter sat across from the Birches and quickly explained why he had suddenly decided to request the bifurcation. It boiled down to the fact that without Don's confession, there were three deaths linked to him by coincidence and circumstantial evidence. The strongest evidence was the eye witness in the Roy Musgrave murder case. When a jury looked at the Scott Miller death alone, without considering any of the evidence of the other cases, the evidence only showed that Scott Miller died because a car fell on him. That could have been Scott's own negligence. Jeff Hays was shot, but there was no direct evidence as to who shot him, even if ballistics came back with a match to Don's .22 pistol that had been recovered the night of the murders.

"So, all we have to do is concentrate on Roy Musgrave's murder after we get the other two cases out of the way."

"How do you plan to defend my husband in that case Mr. Smith?" It was a question that caught Dexter off guard and irritated him.

"I don't know that I can Mrs. Birch. But I will have several months now to try to do just that, without having to focus any attention on the facts in the other cases. Deposing the state's eye witness should help me answer that question for you though."

74

Don Birch was also a little irritated with his wife's question. "Dexter, you just keep doing what you're doing for me. I know I'll get the best there is for me in all this."

Dexter saw the Birches out and locked the door behind them and drew the shades. He looked down at his desk. Things were piling up on him. He had never had a client to take up so much of his time before Don Birch. Dexter needed to spend the next few days catching up on his other cases. He also realized it was time to take Wilbur Pedersen up on his offer to bill the county for extra time on Don's case. Dexter figured what he had done in Don's case over the last few days was about ten hours over what he usually did for the county in a week. That would net him about an extra eight hundred bucks. Dexter thought he could handle this for a while. He also thought that he may need an assistant if it kept up.

8

The next morning, Dexter called Jeremy Wilson and set up an appointment. He needed an update from Jeremy on how things were going before the sentencing hearing in another week. Then, Dexter called around on the Gracie June matter. A team meeting for all the parties in the case was now set and Dexter called Wendel to let them know when and where that would be.

Then, Dexter headed out the door to the courthouse to check his boxes. When he got there, he realized there was a stir of some sort going on. After talking to a couple of people in the courthouse, including the deputy who worked security in the courtrooms, Dexter learned that while he was hard at work that morning, Mildred Pedersen, the County Attorney's own mother, was being cited by law enforcement for third degree assault after she tried to affect a citizen's arrest on a man driving down main street she suspected of driving drunk.

Mildred Pedersen was driving down main street that morning on her way to the Lutheran Church to practice her piano solo and give piano lessons when she noticed that the car in front of her was driving unreasonably slow. She also noticed some swerving and decided that it was some drunk out on the road, obviously a degenerate because it was only nine in the morning. At the next stop light, when the car in front of her did not move after the light had turned green, she stepped out of her own car with the taser she kept for protection since her sons had taken her .32 from her. She opened Bob Schmitt's car door and announced to Bob that he was being placed under citizen's arrest for suspicion of drunk driving. Getting no response, she drive-stunned Bob, but still got no response as poor Bob was already slumped over on the passenger seat in a diabetic coma brought on by ketoacidosis.

As Mildred would later explain it to her friends, it was all a big misunderstanding. But, clearly one her son did not need at the moment. Mildred and her late husband had made big plans for their first-born son. By their calculations, he would be running for congress in another year. This wouldn't help that cause. How dare Bob Schmitt screw it all up like this?

As Dexter understood everything, a grocer from one of the Mexican markets down town had called 911 when he heard car horns honking and Mrs. Pedersen screaming for help. The first deputy on the scene called an ambulance for Mr. Schmitt and ordered Mildred Pedersen to park her own car and then wait on the curb until further notice.

This callous treatment resulted in Mildred calling her son to have the deputy fired. Wilbur, wanting to know for himself what the hell was happening, called the sheriff who personally went to the scene, arriving at the same time as the ambulance crew. Mildred, not wanting things to escalate into an even bigger spectacle, tried to waive off the ambulance crew, insisting that she was alright and not in need of their assistance. Puzzled, the ambulance crew froze in their tracks until the insulant deputy told them to ignore Mrs. Pedersen and assist the poor, comatose driver she had assaulted.

Sheriff Coffee immediately took control, offering the deputy a scowl for the benefit of Mrs. Pedersen and then put the deputy in charge of the scene while he took Mrs. Pedersen to the nearby coffee shop to take her statement and diffuse her involvement.

It really was all one big misunderstanding according to Mildred, once she realized what was actually happening. She did not think that poor Bob Schmitt should be charged for all of this. "After all," she explained. "The stigma of diabetes and not caring for himself was punishment enough."

While Dexter was in County Court getting the low down on all of this, the deputy and Sheriff Coffee were in Wilbur Pedersen's office trying to decide what the hell to do.

"I know that we could cite Bob Schmitt for careless driving and driving while impaired" Wilbur could be heard shouting at Sheriff Coffee and the deputy. "Under normal circumstances I would consider that. But, these are far from normal circumstances. And, that bitch needs to be put in her place, even if she is my mother."

By now, the tension was gone from Wilbur's voice and he calmly looked at the deputy. "And, deputy, you, the primary officer on this case, need to cite her for third degree assault."

"Why me?"

"Because, it's your case. You are the primary officer."

"No sir, I know what something like this could do to my career."

"Look deputy, you are young, she is old, she won't live forever. You will be fine. You have the sheriff and me on your side."

"I know I'll outlive her, but if she outlives the two of you, and she probably will, I'm royally fucked."

"Look, deputy, she is my mother, I love her more than life itself. And, if she should outlive me, you have my permission to drive a stake through her heart and douse her in holy water. Now, get out there, cite her for third degree assault and send the citation here. I will forward it to a special prosecutor as soon as the AG in Lincoln tells me who that will be."

Dexter left the courthouse that day with a couple of appointments on probation violation cases as well as two DUI cases and a new juvenile case. Things got this busy occasionally for him, but it wasn't what he needed right now with the Don Birch case to deal with.

Dexter decided to skip Chinese for lunch and headed down to The Pawnee Club for a sandwich. He had an idea of the gossip that would be circulating there after the morning's events and he was in the mood to be entertained.

Gina brought him a Diet Coke and he ordered a patty melt and onion rings. Then, he sat pretending to contemplate his soda can while he strained to pick up any conversations in the place. Sure enough, at the end of the bar, just a few seats from Dexter, two old guys were talking about Mildred Pedersen and Bob Schmitt. Dexter gathered that both had gone to school with Bob and one was now his neighbor.

The neighbor said that he had seen Bob swaying that morning on his way out to the car. "Hell, it was nine in the morning. I knew he wasn't drunk, besides, Bob has never drunk, to my knowledge."

"I don't think he ever did" the other one cut in. "Even back in high school he wouldn't take a beer if someone offered him one."

"Exactly" the neighbor took over again "He had always had diabetes, so he was always afraid to drink. Anyway, I saw him go to his car and he didn't look right, so I asked was everything alright. He said he had his morning roll and then realized he was almost out of insulin. I offered to drive him, but he said no, he could make it to the drugstore."

"Well, that wouldn't make him pass out like that, would it?"

"Not usually, but he was sick all last week with the flu. Anyway, he's up there getting IVs now and they may keep him over night. That electric shock sure as hell didn't help him none."

"I hate that uppity bitch, what the hell was she thinking?"

"I don't know, but I hope Bob sues her rich ass. But he won't. He's not like that at all."

About that time two old carpenters came in, picking up the last of the conversation. "You guys talking about Bob Schmitt? What the hell was all that about?"

That half of the bar then quieted down so everyone could listen to Bob's neighbor recount the whole thing again so everyone could hear. It was pretty much the same story as Dexter had heard in the courthouse. About halfway through the telling, there was a pause as everyone craned to hear a wail form a distant siren. "Sounds like Mildred's making a run for it" someone said, and they all laughed, and Bob's neighbor resumed his telling.

Food started to come out to the tables. Dexter got his patty melt and The Pawnee Club settled into a quiet hum. Halfway through Dexter's patty melt, as he popped an onion ring into his mouth, the front door flew open and a farmer framed by the noonday sun on his back called out, "You all hear the news?"

"Yeah," Someone said, "That Pedersen lady almost killed Bob Schmitt for driving while diabetic." Everyone laughed.

"No," the farmer said, "Judge Anderson just dropped dead over at the courthouse."

9

Judge James J. Anderson was 68 years-old, 5' 10" tall, and weighed almost 300 pounds. Drinking, eating, golfing and Republican Politics were his passions in life. He was the son, grandson, and great-grandson of the most prominent doctors in the County's history. But, after his third failed attempt at organic chemistry, he switched his major to History and set his sights on law school.

Back at home, he worked a few years for an aging lawyer and then bought the practice from the elder lawyer's widow. Anderson spent most of his attention trying to involve himself in local politics with an eye on the U.S. Congressional Seat for the District. No one in the local Republican Party supported this idea, but he never took the hint. So, for convenience sake, when the preceding County Judge retired, the powers that be saw an opportunity to rid themselves of James Anderson and his meddling in their politics. Everyone agreed that even he would not be stupid enough to turndown an appointment to the County Court Bench.

While his ascension to the bench was convenient to the local politicians, it infuriated the local bar. Most lawyers in the area accepted the appointment in time, even if none had ever truly warmed to it. Behind his back, some called Judge Anderson's Court "the people's court."

It was all for the good of the people, as Judge Anderson saw it. Legal burdens shifted. A long-standing legal precedent may be ignored in a probate case, for the benefit of maintaining good relations among extended family that had always hated each other anyway. A juvenile offender never got any real due process. And, while the lawyers sneered at it all, no one complained or appealed. To do either would risk being taken off the court appointment list and no one could afford to give up those cases, the only cases that were truly guaranteed to pay their legal fees because it was the county paying them.

Dexter headed back to his office after lunch to double check his calendar for that afternoon and the next week, he needed to find out how soon Judge Anderson's death would affect hearings. It was Thursday and Dexter had kept Friday clear to work on the Birch case. As he was in the middle of this, the phone rang. It was Wilbur Pedersen. "Dexter, come over in an hour. I'm getting all the lawyers together in my office to get a handle on this Judge Anderson thing."

Dexter recognized Wilbur's voice right off. Wilbur never announced himself when he called. It always irritated Dexter when people did this. So, Dexter shot back "Who the hell is this?"

"It's Wilbur Pedersen, you know god-damn good and well who it is. Now stop screwing around and get your fat ass over here in an hour. Actually, come about fifteen minutes early."

Wilbur talked like this occasionally, but only when he was really irritated. Dexter was usually proud of himself for pushing Wilbur's buttons, but the "fat ass" thing stung just a little. Dexter had only one thing on the calendar for the afternoon, a county court probation violation hearing. He called the client and told him there would be no court because there was now no judge. He hung up the phone and headed over to Wilbur's office early because there was simply nothing else to do.

When Dexter got to Wilbur's office, Wilbur's staff let Dexter know that he was too early, and Wilbur was with someone. They didn't say Wilbur was with someone more important, but Dexter knew it was implied. Wilbur's office door was closed. Dexter waited. About ten minutes before the meeting was to start, Dexter was still the only attorney there. Wilbur's door opened, his head popped out and darted around until his eyes landed on Dexter. "Get in here."

Dexter made his way around the counter and across the wooden floor, through the short maze of staff desks and mix-matched file cabinets and into Wilbur's office. Wilbur was already back in his big chair behind his desk and Tom McWilliams was on the love seat. "Shut the door and grab a seat."

Dexter moved to one of the large conference chairs in front of the desk and turned it so he could face between the other two men.

"Before we start, I want to give you this." Wilbur handed Dexter a check made out to Dexter for $1500. Dexter looked at it, looked at Tom, who was looking down at the floor, then looked to Wilbur. "What's this?"

"My mother got herself into a pickle this morning. I have told her that you are going to represent her."

Dexter did not know what to say. Dexter was not sure how to feel about this. He looked to Tom McWilliams for help, but Tom was still staring at the floor.

"My mother expects the best. And right now, after what you have done for Don Birch, you are the best criminal attorney around.

"I have to hand it to you Dexter. I expected you to find Bod Anderson's colossal blunder on the confession. I would have been disappointed in you if you had missed it. But, that motion to bifurcate, that was a real haymaker you snuck into my blindside. So, you are the best lawyer in town and my mother will have you representing her. Besides, with the Judge dying, there won't be so much attention on her around town."

Dexter was flattered, still, he could not pass up the opening he was just given, "You don't think she had anything to do with it, do you?"

Wilbur and Tom both gave Dexter a puzzled look, "You know, your mother, you don't think she knocked-off the Judge to divert attention from what she did this morning?"

Tom McWilliams buried his face into his open hands and shook convulsively. Wilbur, though annoyed, did manage to see the humor in what Dexter had just done, "Is that any way to talk about a paying client?" is all he could manage by way of reply.

"Look, there is one other thing here we need to talk about before the others get here. And, it need not leave this room just yet. Now, I saw the extra hours you submitted to the county, that's good. We want Don to get adequate counsel here. Judge Anderson was the only one who ever really picked those claims apart anyway."

Wilbur trailed off a little, searching for just the right words. "Look Dexter. I want to put in for the county judgeship. It is really all I want to do at this point in my life. I see no reason why I won't get it if I apply. So, we will need a new county attorney. Neither of my deputies have enough experience and neither of them want to stay around here. That is where Tom here comes in."

Tom now took over, "You see, Dexter, I've made it no secret that I want to be the next District Court Judge. Ostergart has said that he will retire in about five more years, if he doesn't die first. The county attorney's office would be much easier to transition to the bench from, if I do get appointed to the bench one day. Closing a private practice takes time and can be a pain in the ass. But, if I am the county attorney, I can take my time and close out my private civil work over the next couple of years from here."

All of this was clear as mud to Dexter, he looked back to Wilbur now. "That's great, but what do I have to do with any of this? And, what about your family's big plans of you running for congress and turning this office over to your son?"

Wilbur was irritated again. "Look, I don't care what my mother tells people or what she and my late father thought I should do. I never wanted to be a congressman and Charlie will certainly never want to come back here after law school.

And after her vigilante crap this morning, she won't dare try to push me around for a while. Hell, I can even act like I am having to settle for a county judgeship because she has ruined my reputation too badly to run for office now."

Tom and Dexter both tried to hold back their laughter. Nothing and no one could get under Wilbur's skin like his mother could. But, no one else dare be so critical of her in his presence. He was, at heart, a momma's boy through and through.

"Look Dexter, we may be putting the cart before the horse here. But, I don't see anyone with a better shot at being judge who would want it. So, Tom and I want to start getting things in order now, not six months from now when a new judge will be seated. Tom needs to cancel his contract with the county now to avoid conflicts when the time comes, and he needs to get this Musgrave estate settled. So, before we talk to John Miller, we want to see how you feel about things."

Tom saw that Dexter was still confused as to why they were telling him about all of this and cut in again. "I've got a one third contract with the county just like yours and John's for public defender work. I've also got a bigger private practice than I can bring into this office. No one else in the area wants my contract and there are no new lawyers coming in right now. So, do you want my contract, or do you want my private work? Or, do you want a little of both?"

Dexter sat there. He had to let all this sink in. He had liked how things had always been. A month ago, he would not have wanted any change. But, the Birch case had changed him, giving him confidence and a desire to do more than just get by for once. He could still become the guy he thought he was going to be when he started law school. But, he would need a staff. He would need to earn enough to pay the added overhead, it was risky. He had to stay in his comfort zone. He had to go with less risk. "So, what would this new county contract look like?"

"Well, you'd get two thirds of all court appointments instead of one third. You would get about sixty thousand a year instead of thirty."

"I don't know, I think this would take more than just my time."

Wilbur just looked at Tom, who nodded in agreement with Dexter.

"OK, Dex, what do you think it should look like?"

Dexter contemplated this for a moment, he hadn't ever given it any serious thought, but, he knew some things that maybe he wasn't supposed to know. "Well, give me forty-five thousand a year, five hundred a month for extra overhead and a secretary on the county payroll."

"And what does she get?"

"Oh, how about twenty-five hours a week, eleven bucks an hour and county health insurance?"

Wilbur looked at Tom, who nodded. Tom's contract had always had a few extra perks that no one was supposed to know about. Wilbur thought it odd that what Dexter was asking for would not really have an effect on the county's budget. He also thought Dexter had come up with those figures pretty quickly. Wilbur gave Tom a raised eyebrow, and let it go.

"OK, I have to meet with the commissioners after this meeting anyway, to fill them in on the judge stuff. I will go see if the others are here yet."

Wilbur opened his office door and ushered in the others he had summoned. John Miller was the first through the door. He gave Dexter and Tom a surprised and slightly hurt look. He knew something was up and he had been left out. Tom would smooth it all over after the meeting by presenting John with a list of surplus clients. Sheriff Coffee and the local State Patrol sergeant walked in next. Behind them, two other lawyers who spent a fair amount of time in the local courthouse, followed by the local supervisor for Health and Human Services.

Wilbur didn't waste any time, "Look, this was a shock to all of us, Judge Anderson dying this morning. Although, he wasn't a pillar of good health and clean living, so maybe we should have seen this coming." This seemed an odd and callous thing to say, even for Wilbur. Strange looks ricocheted around the room. "I don't mean to seem crass, but we need to be practical about how things are going to run until we get a new judge."

"Any idea when that will be?" Asked the state trooper.

"No, but it usually takes six months. Give or take." Some of the older lawyers in the room nodded their heads in agreement with Wilbur.

"Who is gonna want it?" John Miller asked.

"Who knows?" Wilbur lied, "But someone will, and in the meantime, the court administrator called me from Lincoln as soon as he heard the news. They are already working on a rotation for other county judges to come and fill-in. It will take a week to get up and running. To start, they will have a judge here on Mondays and Fridays. If that won't do, they will try to add an extra day here and there."

Wilbur explained that for the time being, the lawyers should try to avoid continuing cases if they could, or scheduling things at the last minute. Visiting judges were providing a courtesy and things should run as smoothly as possible for them. Judge Ostergart had already promised to not schedule hearings in District Court on Mondays and Fridays, unless the attorneys asked for them.

"We need to keep jail arraignments to a minimum." Wilbur was looking at the sheriff and the state patrol sergeant now. "So, whenever possible, cite offenders into court. If it's a DWI and they have a sober friend or relative to come and get them, just cite them and let them go. Domestic assault, cite the guy and send him to a relative's house to stay, unless the victim has to go to the hospital."

Now, Wilbur spoke directly to the sergeant, "You and your men aren't going to like this, but I'll need you to lay off looking for drug runners passing through. If it looks bad, tail them into the next county if you can and make the stop." The sergeant bristled. He and his men would sooner stop taking shits or breathing. They lived for the "non-profiling" profiling. Find someone who doesn't look right and follow them until they made the slightest traffic infraction, stop them and look for any probable cause to search. Cross the center line, go a mile-per-hour over the speed limit, fail to signal a full one hundred feet before turning or changing lanes and bam. "Hello, where you headed? Where you been? Mind if I search your vehicle? You do? Well, I think I detect an odor of marijuana, so please step out of the car and wait in my patrol unit." Or, maybe they just think the driver looks nervous, sweaty, twitchy eyes. "Just sit here while I run my dog around your car." Most state troopers had been Marines first. They lived for action.

So, yeah, the sergeant minded this request. Never mind that most of these people they caught were running pot or other drugs through the country from California to New York or Chicago. They were just passing through. The way the defense lawyers all saw it, it wasn't a Nebraska problem. Why clog the Nebraska courts?

"My troopers won't like that one bit."

"I know sergeant. But it is temporary. If someone is obviously breaking the law, do what you have to do. But, if it is just a hunch and your guys want to follow them a while, just follow them into the next county before you stop them. It is just temporary. And, it will be appreciated."

Wilbur finally turned to the Social Services supervisor and asked that kids be left at home with services in the home, unless there was a serious safety concern. "If there are any questions, call me; day or night. I will help out however I can. If it's life or death or a risk of serious bodily harm, pull the kids and we will just get a judge here for the out of home placement hearings."

When the meeting broke up, Dexter headed down to The Pawnee Club. "I'll have a beer Sam. And, when does Gina come in?"

"She should be here about five. Why?"

"I need to hire her."

****

Gina was skeptical of Dexter's offer at first. She had always found him a little creepy. But she found most men his age creepy. He had never made a pass at her or anything. If anything, it was a seeming androgyny to the man she found odd. She had heard some people speculate that he was gay. Others speculated that he had an autism spectrum disorder that made him a little different. All in all, she knew he was harmless, and the more he told her about the job, the better it sounded. Twenty-five hours a week at eleven bucks an hour would be steadier income than she was getting anywhere else. But, that county health insurance, that was what made the offer something Gina could not pass up. She held a poker face though, for just long enough to get a little extra.

"I have bookkeeping clients. I want to use your office to do their work. Not on your time, but I need space." She paused a moment to mull over her one other demand. "And, I won't take shit from people. I know what kinds of people you represent. I have to take their shit, to a point, when I serve them in here. I won't take it if I am working for you."

Dexter had his own reservations about hiring Gina. She had been the first person to come to his mind, mainly because advertising for and interviewing candidates just seemed like work beyond Dexter's patience. But, Gina was an odd duck. Dexter never knew if she was shy, or just kind of a bitch. Did she have any personality? He honestly had never seen any sign of one from her. Gina being Sam's niece was a double-edged sword too. Sure, it probably meant she was a good egg, but at the same time, if he ever had to fire

89

her, how would Sam take it? Still, she was smart, she was a bookkeeper and probably more than competent to do the job. At the same time, with that hair and her eccentricities, Dexter knew there was a good chance he would be far less self-conscious with her than any other qualified candidate. Having weighed all this in his mind before he even offered her the job, Dexter knew she was the only realistic option for him.

Dexter pretended to consider Gina's counter demands for a moment. "I think that is more than reasonable." And he and Gina shook ceremoniously, both pretending not to take the old ritual seriously. And with that, Dexter had a legal staff for the first time in his career. Things were temporarily grinding to a halt with Judge Anderson's death, so Dexter and Gina agreed that she would start the day after the funeral.

Dexter went back to his office, he had two voice mails. One was from Don Birch. The other was from his newest client, Mildred Pedersen. Dexter returned both calls and set appointments with each client on the following Monday.

Dexter spent the next day, Friday, pouring through reports on the Don Birch case. He had a list of witnesses with notes on each one. He went through social media on the internet trying to find all he could on each of them. It wasn't much.

There were a couple of things staring Dexter in the face. For starters, the witness in the Roy Musgrave murder had Don Birch at Musgrave's dealership at the same time Jeff Hays' neighbor claimed to have heard a gunshot. For another, rumors were becoming more rampant that Jeff's wife, Linda, Jr., was spending more and more time with Will Jorgensen.

The discrepancy in time could be explained away. It had been drilled into every law student, including Dexter, that once a thing is done, the facts of it are lost forever. With ten eye-witnesses to an event come ten different versions of the event. Still, it would work in Dexter's favor at trial. Anything that created any reasonable doubt should be pounced on by the defense.

It could have just been a mistake in notetaking by a deputy. That happened sometimes. There was just one way to settle it. Dexter picked up the phone and called Wilbur.

Wilbur was in a pretty good mood when his secretary put Dexter's call through to him. "Well, surprised to get a call from you on a Friday afternoon. Have you ever worked on a Friday afternoon before?"

"Not since I took the bar exam. Will, we need to start depositions on this Birch case. There is no way we can do them all in one day. I'm not even sure who all I need to depose, but I think it will be several days' worth. What do you think about them?"

"I agree entirely. Let's go get coffee somewhere and start sorting it out. I have the cases split out now, thanks to your motion to bifurcate. The new informations have all the endorsed witnesses listed on each case. There is a lot of overlap, but there are a few witnesses that only appear on one case or the other. Why don't you meet me down at the diner in twenty minutes? Bring your calendar and your witness list and we'll figure this out."

Dexter didn't have a list of his own witnesses yet. He started running through potential witnesses in his head, but most of his witnesses, besides his own client, who couldn't be deposed and may not even testify, would probably already be listed as the state's witnesses.

He sat in the café for about five minutes before Wilbur came in and sat across from him. Wilbur handed Dexter a manila envelope "Here are your new informations."

Dexter took them out and saw two separate District Court informations captioned with two different case numbers, each charging Donald Birch with a single count of first degree murder. One was for the murder of Roy Musgrave, the other for the murder of Jeff Hays. Dexter looked back in the envelope and then up at Wilbur. "Where is the one for Scott Miller?"

"You know I can't prove that one now. How many life without parole sentences do I really need to stack up against your client anyway? Besides, I can always file it down the road if something turns up. No statute of limitations on murder." It was one of those things no lawyer needed to be told, but prosecutors loved to point out anyway.

They each ordered coffee and a piece of pie. Then the two went over the potential witnesses for the state. Dexter confessed that he had no independent witnesses for the defense yet, but both agreed that it was probably too early in the game to have those anyway. He needed to see more of the State's case before his own would come into focus.

"I'm gonna want to depose Jeff's neighbor first, Joe Freisen. And the guy who spotted Don at Roy's office. And, Bob Anderson and any other deputies who spoke to those two."

"You want to depose Bob Anderson? You've already cross-examined him at the suppression hearing. He's gonna be sore as hell with you if you keep rubbing the illegal confession in his face."

"I will keep that in mind and try not to go there. I just don't like their timing. These two, the neighbor and the janitor at the car lot put Don at both crime scenes at the same time."

"Yeah, you know, that was my only problem when this was one case. Now that there are two, I can argue two conflicting theories in front of separate juries, no problem at all."

Dexter mulled this over, it was true, but Dexter could still work it to his advantage. And, who said he was going to ask for juries to hear the cases?

They went through the list quickly, picked the six most pertinent witnesses to start with and set some dates.

"The commissioners agreed to your contract proposals. You find a secretary yet?"

"Yeah, she will start the middle of next week. I will bring her up and introduce her when I show her around the courthouse."

"The county clerk knows you are getting someone. Take her over there to do her employee paperwork. John Miller didn't take the news of your contract too hard. Tom is going to resign his positions as attorney for the school district and the hospital board. He promised to recommend John for those."

"Well, maybe I should have held out for those and let John take the extra public defender work."

"Really, you want to represent boards?" Wilbur tried to pose this as a serious question, but the mental image he had of Dexter sitting through hospital board meetings, answering tedious questions about employment and administrative law was just too much. Dexter backed down when he saw Wilbur's smirk.

"No. I can't see myself doing that." Dexter said, getting a mental image of himself not unlike Wilbur's. "This will suit me fine."

"Has my mother called you?"

"Yep, we have an appointment Monday."

"OK, the AG has appointed a special prosecutor. He will file the complaint on Monday. They are also going to have their own investigator come out and review what the deputies did and get a second statement from Mr. Schmidt." All kinds of puns and jokes about Mildred Pedersen and her shocking behavior ran through Dexter's head. He held them back. He was grateful that Wilbur had enough respect and trust in him to let him represent Mildred.

Dexter walked back with Wilbur towards the courthouse as far as his own office. There, it occurred to him that the khaki Dickies and hopsack blazer he wore most days would probably not do for the cases to come. He had that one new suit he had worn to the suppression hearing, but he would need one or two more.

He got online and checked eBay. There were plenty of guys out there his size who had gotten a nice suit, worn it once to a cousin's wedding or a funeral, and lost a bunch of weight and was selling it now online. There were plenty of estates selling clothes too. The fact is, unless they are bankers, lawyers, or administrators of some sort, most men didn't wear a suit enough times to ware it out.

Dexter found two he liked in his size. They were both five hundred-dollar suits, and he paid about fifty for each with shipping. What could possibly go wrong with that?

10

The special prosecutor for the AG's office prosecuting Mildred Pedersen faxed Dexter a copy of the complaint he intended to file first thing Monday morning. It charged her with one count of third degree assault. That was a class one misdemeanor. This was very generous considering the facts easily supported felony charges. A note attached said that the investigator had talked to Mr. Schmidt by telephone already and Mr. Schmidt did not see any point in making too big a deal of the situation.

Dexter put the documents in Mrs. Pedersen's file and started a pot of coffee. The Birches would be in soon. He wondered what they wanted. Clients were either a pain in the ass by never contacting you, or they were pains in the ass by constantly contacting you. There was rarely an in-between. The Birches were probably going to be the latter. Of course, given the seriousness of Don's cases, it was probably not a bad thing.

Both Birches turned down Dexter's offer for coffee, having already had their morning cups. Linda was very anxious to get down to business, wanting to know all the next steps in the case. She also wanted to know if Judge Anderson's death would have any bearing on the case.

"No ma'am, not directly anyway. If anything, it could free me up more in the coming weeks to work on Don's case. We will only have a visiting judge a couple of days a week, so I won't be in court so much.

"That will be the only effect on Don's case because his case is in District Court."

"You mean cases, don't you? You had the cases all divided out, right? So, there are three cases now."

"Actually, there are only two cases. Without a confession, there is no evidence that Scott Miller's death was anything but an accident. So, there are just two cases, and Wilbur

Pedersen will have to show how Don was in two places at once."

This confused the Birches, so Dexter walked them through the timelines that showed he was seen at Roy's office at the same time Jeff's neighbor heard gunshots.

The Birches both went a little white when they heard this. Dexter was sure this would please them. Maybe this was how they showed it. Dexter was having a hell of a time reading these people.

"What does this mean Mr. Smith?" Linda Birch wanted to know.

"Well, it probably just means that someone was confused about the time that night. But, it could help us create a little reasonable doubt. That is all we have to do, create doubt about what happened. Does it mean anything to either of you? You both look a little uneasy."

"Oh, no. No." Linda said as she looked to Don who was now shrugging it all off. "No, it just seemed odd."

Dexter and the Birches went over the list of witnesses Dexter and Wilbur would be deposing and then they decided to set a standing appointment every Monday at 9:30 for the time being. Dexter then walked them to the door to see them out as Mildred Pedersen met them, coming in for her appointment. She was eight minutes early.

"Hello Linda, Don."

"Hello Mildred." Linda answered with a forced smile. The two women engaged in a quick hug and released. The Birches walked out, and Dexter showed Mildred Pedersen into the office. Dexter was rigid, trying ridiculously to be formal, or in some way different with Mrs. Pedersen. Mrs. Pedersen smiled casually like Dexter was an old friend and took the chair he offered her.

"Mr. Smith, I don't think my cousin was overly happy to see me, do you?"

"I beg your pardon."

"Linda, she didn't seem glad to see me. I think she hates me. I enjoy being nice to her every chance I get. I know, it's petty, but I just can't help myself." Mildred Pedersen now reminded Dexter of the cheerleaders he knew in high school who pretended to be friends with people when they needed something from someone, even if it was just attention, or someone to talk to when they were stuck in a class with none of their regular friends.

"Linda Birch is your cousin?"

"Why yes, our mothers were first cousins. We were always close growing up. She was a junior bridesmaid in my wedding."

This knocked Dexter back a little. But, there was a similarity in the women. It was almost like Linda Birch was a cheap imitation of Mildred Pedersen when he compared them in his mind. Mildred was a little colder and more refined. Linda a little more stern and severe. So, why was Wilbur prosecuting Don with this family conflict?

"I had no idea. I am surprised Wilbur would prosecute Don if they are related."

"Oh, I don't think it even occurs to Wilbur. We have never been close to them since Linda and Donald were married. Even before really. My father and Linda's grandfather had farming interests together that went better for my father than it did for her grandfather. So, now there are resentments even though no one knows anymore exactly what happened.

"Linda followed me everywhere when she was a child. I taught her piano. My parents helped pay for her college. I always gave her my nicest clothes, when I was finished with them. I think she hates me for that.

"You know Mr. Smith, sometimes I believe that kindness is the hardest thing in the world to forgive. People and their silly pride."

Dexter sat and nodded. There was something in Mildred Pedersen to be awed.

"Well. Now. Mr. Smith, what are you going to do about my embarrassing little situation? Do you think you can handle the special prosecutor for me the way you have handled my son for Donald Birch?"

Dexter knew that Mildred Pedersen was only being slightly patronizing. She seemed to have some real confidence in him, and he truly appreciated it. "Well, Mrs. Pedersen, I guess this all depends on what you want to happen. Do you want to fight this, or do you want to quietly work something out and move on?"

"Well, I don't like the idea of having a criminal record. But, I like the idea of a trial even less. It was a misunderstanding after all. I just want it to go away as quietly and as painlessly as possible.

"I am just thankful that James Anderson dropped stone dead when he did. That spiteful, stupid man would have put me in jail for sure if he had been given the chance."

"Well, Mrs. Pedersen. I think this will all be relatively painless. I assume you don't have any prior assaults on your record." Dexter meant this as a joke but regretted saying it as soon as it came out of his mouth. Would she really appreciate such a joke?

Mildred Pedersen gave an icy stare as she pursed her lips together and Dexter suddenly felt sick to his stomach. The ice in Mrs. Pedersen's eyes was melted by the wry smile that grew across her face. She could not hold it back any further. "Oh, Mr. Smith, no. No, I have never been *convicted* of anything before now. I guess I am getting careless in my old age."

Dexter laughed, partly at the joke she had made, but mostly out of relief she wasn't offended by his.

"I agree that this will be relatively painless. Relatively." Mildred allowed the dramatic pause to have its effect before continuing. "Why, even Mr. Schmidt wants all of this to just go away. We visited about it yesterday."

"You saw Bob Schmidt yesterday?"

"Yes, I found a recipe for some sugarless cookies, of all things, and took him a batch. He really is a very nice man, and he has quite recovered from all of this. I like to think I helped him by bringing his condition to everyone's attention so quickly. He had no business driving when he was in that condition. But, we mustn't judge him too harshly for that."

"No. No ma'am, we shouldn't" was all the response Dexter could muster. Dexter was having a hard time wrapping his head around an idea that Bob Schmidt was somehow to blame for any of this.

"Mr. Smith. I do a great deal of work for many organizations and causes in this community. I am from one of the best families in this county and I married into THE best family. I can't imagine anyone being too interested in sending me to the big house. I am sure you will be able to work something out that will satisfy me."

"Yes, well, I do have the police reports and statements here." Dexter was used to clients wanting to look over such things with him.

"I have seen those Mr. Smith. They are what they are. You must let me know what you and the special prosecutor work out.

"Now, I have to go to the church and help get ready for Judge Anderson's funeral. We are expecting at least two hundred, and the church will probably have to feed two thirds of them after the burial."

11

When any lawyer dies, the local bar is expected to give a nice send-off. A judge, even James Anderson, must get a little more. The ceremonies started on Monday afternoon with visitation. Lawyers and judges from all over the state were there, along with bankers, court clerks, traveling court reporters, and law enforcement from throughout the region. The Governor sent a wreath, as did the attorney general. Most of the out of town big shots would not make it back for the funeral the next day so they made sure to be seen at the visitation.

When the visitation broke-up, a handful of the attorneys who had practiced most in the area found themselves together at a table in the back of The Pawnee Club. This group included Dexter, Wilbur, Tom McWilliams, and John Miller. It was kind of an exclusive party in a very public place. It irritated some of the regular patrons who didn't come to The Pawnee Club on a week night to be made to feel self-conscious by the local bar association taking over the place like a wild pack of drunken frat boys invading a blue-collar bar on the edge of a college town.

The frat pack was completely without restraint and seemed oblivious to anyone else in the place, except for Gina, who was serving them. This made Dexter uneasy, so he made it a point to introduce Gina as his new assistant and bookkeeper before one of the others might happen to make a lewd comment about her. To Dexter's surprise, Wilbur and Tom both vouched for Gina's skills and congratulated Dexter on the good hire. Both had regularly done taxes for some of the people she kept books for, and they were impressed with her work. Tom had even referred some people to her for bookkeeping work. This all made Dexter feel much better, but he was still a little self-conscious in the group. This was his bar, the regulars in the place were his friends. How would they all feel about him after seeing him with this group?

Pat Blocker and Teddy Pickrell were at the end of the bar, closest to the group. Pat was throwing back his amaretto and Sprite as quickly as Teddy was slamming his PBRs, which was always fast. The more the lawyers drank, the more irreverent they became about the memory of Judge James Anderson. Each of the lawyers had two or three stories about bad rulings the Judge had made in cases they had with him, or tirades he had unleashed on them from the bench in front of their clients, and packed courtrooms. There were stories about awkward social situations after the Judge had drunk a little too much from time to time. By ten p.m. with everyone good and hammered, the really nasty talk started; stories of the Judge's boorish treatment of his own family and extramarital activities were fair game.

Pat and Teddy listened raptly. The alcohol was dissolving the imagined social burrier between the two at the bar and attorneys. Pat and Teddy began laughing louder and louder at what the lawyers were saying about the Judge. They had by now turned completely around on their stools to listen, but were being politely ignored. It was getting to be too much for Dexter. He wished Pat and Teddy would go away before their feelings were hurt.

Finally, Phil Taft, an older lawyer who had gone to law school with the Judge and outright hated the Judge, turned to Teddy. "Aren't you one of Bob Pickrell's kids?"

"Yep. I'm Teddy Pickrell."

"Well, Teddy, how many times do you think ol' Judge Anderson sent your dad to jail? Hell, didn't he even send some of you kids to Boys' Town a few times?"

Teddy Pickrell, for all his faults, was not his father. Bob Pickrell was a mean, thieving drunk who never did anything good for anyone but himself, least of all his wife and kids. The lawyers in town may not have had much good to say about Teddy, he was a bum. But, he was their bum, and Phil

Taft hadn't practiced in the area in some time. He was about to cross a line as far as everyone else at the table was concerned. But, Teddy appreciated attention, any attention.

"Yep, Mr. Taft. You represented me a few times when I was a juvenile. I always thought Judge Anderson had it in for me, especially when I was a teenager. He probably thought the apple didn't fall too far from the tree. But, I probably wouldn't have finished high school if I hadn't got caught up on credits at Boys' Town. It got me away from my dad too.

"But, you know what I remember most about the Judge? I remember my dad taking me to court with him on Halloween when I was six. He was getting sentenced for stealing a case of beer and punching the liquor store clerk who was trying to block the door.

"My dad took me along cause he thought the Judge wouldn't send him to jail with me there. He begged for probation and asked what would happen to me if he went to jail and couldn't take me back to school. Then he started talking about how he wanted to take me to the dollar store and get me a Halloween costume after court and all. Man, I sure got fired up when he said that, I had no idea he was planning on doing that. I had never been trick-or-treating before.

"Well, the Judge saw through all that and it just made him madder at my dad. So, he sent my dad to jail for two months and had a deputy drive me back to school. Of course, I didn't see through it and I was pissed that the Judge had ruined my Halloween.

"But then, when I was walking home from school that afternoon, I looked up and here comes his big ol Lincoln toward me, pulling over into the wrong lane, and it pulls up right alongside of me there on the sidewalk and out pops this big hand holding a plastic Frankenstein costume. Shoved it right into my hands and that car just tore out of there. Took me a minute to realize it was the Judge and what he was doing and all. That was the only time I had a Halloween costume to trick-or-treat in until Pat and I got to be friends and his parents would get me costumes."

The attorneys were all quietly looking at Teddy now as he took a breath, and grinned up at Phil Taft. "So, I see what you were getting at Mr. Taft. And yep, Judge Anderson was a first-class son-of-a-bitch alright. But, I don't think he was the worst son-of-a-bitch I ever knew."

"Gina," yelled Tom McWilliams, "we need another round, it's my turn to buy. And get Teddy and Pat whatever they're drinking."

And with that, Pat and Teddy were invited to join the grown-ups' table. For the rest of the night, the two entertained the piss drunk lawyers with sophomoric sex and fart jokes. A couple of the lawyers reminisced about Pat's grandfather, who had truly been respected by all of them. Pat beamed at these until he started to get weepy, and the fart jokes started back again to change the subject. They all laughed until they were kicked out at closing time when it suddenly hit them that they had to be at a funeral in nine hours.

****

Dexter's alarm went off at 7:30 and by 7:38 he was awake enough to hit the snooze bar. The funeral was at ten and Dexter knew it would take every ounce of his fortitude to make it to the funeral and back home to sleep off the rest of the day. By 8:20 Dexter had no idea how many times he had hit the snooze bar, but he knew he would have to get up very soon, not just to get ready but to almost certainly throw-up. He also had to pee.

He started to push himself off the couch, but that sent a pain into his head and limbs. So, Dexter dragged himself off the couch and crawled toward the bathroom. The closer to the bathroom he got, the more he feared not making it in time. He felt eruptions percolating from every orifice. He knew the sneeze was the most dangerous. That would set everything else off all at once. It was no longer a matter of making it to the bathroom in time. It was making to the tile floor of the bathroom where cleanup would be manageable. As he made it to the bathroom door, he began pulling at his shorts, crawling out of them as he crawled along the bathroom floor to the toilet. The cold of the tile was a relief and he threw his body over and into the tub as he stuck his head into the toilet. He waited.

It was the sneeze, just as he had suspected. It came upon him with sudden violence. It was deep and loud. It convulsed him and immediately he felt the hot water shooting out of his ass just as quickly, loudly and violently as the sneeze had been. Yes, he was shitting in his bathtub, more of a shotgun like blast that painted the side of the big tub a yellowish brown, and before he could react to any of this, he wretched. A torrent of fluids and chunks of he knew not what exploded out of his mouth and nose. As quickly as the first one ended, a second one hit. This one stuck with him a while as his stomach muscles involuntarily strained. He could not breathe, he needed the contraction to end so that he could breathe. He did not want to be found dead like this. Finally, it let up and he took two deep breaths before the next one hit. It lasted even longer, though it was producing nothing. He was empty now. He just waited for it to end. It was followed by three more empty wretches each ending just a little more quickly than the last. Dexter waited for bile and blood to come, but they never did.

Dexter hovered there, half in the bathtub and his head in the toilet, until the small hit. It was a smell of death. Every ounce of bodily fluid his body could spare had been evacuated and it filled his nostrils. He suspected people who had been found dead after several days smelled like this. It was an acrid, putrefying smell. He reached up and flushed. That helped some. He turned the water on in his big, claw footed tub and grabbed the hose with the shower head on the end and washed most of that mess out of the tub. Nothing solid had come out of that end. He washed it all down the drain.

Dexter sat back in the tub and stopped it up. He started drinking from the shower head to quench the fire now blazing between his ears and down in his gut. The worst was over, he hoped.

Dexter soaked in the tub for as long as he could. He finally pulled and plug and climbed out with fifty minutes to spare until the funeral began. He went and found the new grey suit he had worn to Don Birch's suppression hearing. He could not stand the thought of a tie, so he found a black polo and put it on over a white T.

He made it to the church with five minutes to spare. Halfway up the right side of the church were two pews reserved for lawyers and judges. The second of the reserved pews was filled by the group Dexter had been with the night before. They all looked up at Dexter with the same self-loathing on their faces that he was feeling.

Wilbur Pedersen was clutching the arm rest on the aisle. He looked up at Dexter and shifted his knees to let Dexter move past him, making it clear that he was not giving up this seat on the end. The rest of the group all scooted down to make room for Dexter. He sat between Wilbur and Tom McWilliams.

Dexter looked up just long enough to see Mildred Pedersen glaring at him and the others on his row from the front, left side of the church. She was sitting with the other church ladies behind the pallbearers. No one in the group of shame spoke, none of them looked up. Dexter alternated between keeping his eyes shut and staring at the tip of his shoe as he vaguely listened to the buzz of conversation around him. Anyone who did not know better might think the lawyers were all grief stricken over the loss of their great Judge.

The music started and they all pulled themselves up to stand and the family filed in. When the family was seated, everyone else sat. The place was packed.

The minister got up, led the mourners in prayer and was about to start the service when a look came over his face. The quiet was finally realized by the hung-over lawyers who all looked up to see that everyone else had turned to look at the door at the back of the church. They too finally turned and saw what everyone else was staring at. It was Pat and Teddy. They stood there, Burger Hut caps in hand, with their Burger Hut polo shirts buttoned all the way up. Pat wore one of his grandfather's old bolo ties. They were frozen, seeing nowhere to sit and not knowing what to do.

"Wilbur, Wilbur." It was a loud whisper coming from the front of the church. Dexter and Wilbur both turned to find that the source of the sound was Mildred Pedersen. She was motioning with her head toward the two at the back of the church, expecting Wilbur to handle the situation. Wilbur, clearly irritated with his mother, pulled himself up from the pew by his coveted armrest and made his way to the back of the church. He pulled Pat and Teddy close to him and spoke quickly to them, nodding his head. The other two nodded their heads, looking down in embarrassment and shame. Wilbur extended his arm forward and the two started walking forward with Wilbur falling in behind them. They made it to the pew of shame and the lawyers started scooting down to make room for them. As Dexter sat up to move his knees and let the two slide past him, he saw a scowl on the face of Mildred Pedersen he will never forget. This was not, apparently, how she had intended for her son to handle the situation. Pat and Teddy settled in between Tom McWilliams and John Miller and the service resumed. Dexter turned to Wilbur who managed a wicked grin through all the pain he was feeling. Wilbur Pedersen's mommy issues never ceased to amaze Dexter.

With everyone settled back down, the minister said a few words and introduced the Judge's niece who sang "On the Wings of A Snow White Dove." Dexter and the others kept their heads down and in a fit of religious fervor, began praying to God that the service would end soon so they could all go home and sleep.

The song was over, the eulogy was half over, God please let it be at least half over. None of them listened to any of it. Dexter looked down at Tom's watch, not having one of his own, and saw it was ten thirty. It had to be more than half over. Funerals don't go an hour. Dexter's head and stomach burned. He was still nauseated and desperately wanted to sleep.

Dexter couldn't tell you who sang the closing hymn or what it was or when it had started. He just realized that it was almost over, and the closing prayer would be next. It was in that very moment of silence, between the end of the closing hymn and the start of the closing prayer that it happened.

A rumble? A groan? A small earthquake? What was that? Did he hear it or feel it, or both?

Dexter looked up. The lawyers in the row ahead of them had all turned to look. Dexter looked to Will, who was looking past Dexter. Dexter turned and looked to the center of the pew. All eyes were on Teddy Pickrell, who stared at the floor, face turning red and tears welling in his eyes. Pat Blocker had a grin on his face that looked like it would erupt with laughter at any moment. The minister started the closing prayer. Pat's smile turned to a look of revulsion in an instant and John Miller clapped his hand over his nose and mouth. The preacher kept praying. Tom McWilliams grabbed his nose and mouth and turned his head to face Dexter. It was then that Dexter realized what had happened as both of his nostrils were assaulted with a smell far worse than what he had smelled that morning in his own bathroom. It was a smell of dead racoon, rotten eggs and PBR. Teddy Pickrell had released one of his infamous beer farts.

At that moment, Dexter believed in God. It was divine intervention that had told Dexter to wear that polo and not a shirt and tie. As he grabbed for the collars of the polo and his undershirt to pull them over his face, Wilbur Pedersen, hit suddenly with the smell, let out an involuntary gasp which drew almost as much attention as the fart itself had.

The preacher prayed louder, the people around Teddy in all directions moaned in unison, and Dexter vomited down the inside of his shirt loudly, purging what little water he now had on his stomach. The preacher said a quick and loud "amen." The organ started playing and everyone stood.

Dexter pinched his nose and the corners of his mouth with his shirt and pulled it down, cleaning off the vomit. They all stared down in shame as the Judge's family was ushered out of the church. The widow paused by them long enough to register her disgust.

The mourners were all dismissed, row by row, all of them stopping to glare. When the ushers got to that row, they passed it by, not even looking at Wilbur or any of the others. Soon, the church was empty but their row. The smell had not dissipated much, so they moved to the back of the church to wait. They waited until they were sure everyone else had left the parking lot and filed out, without a word between any of them.

Dexter made his way home. He threw his shirts into the washing machine, grabbed two Diet Cokes from the fridge, got his cigarettes and climbed into the tub for a long soak. He would sleep away the rest of the day. Gina was starting in the morning.

12

Having slept off some of his shame and most of his pain, Dexter was out of bed, showered and dressed by eight thirty. He headed down stairs to find Gina sitting in her car out front, smoking a cigarette and listening to the radio. When she saw him, Gina flicked the cigarette out of her window, rolled it up and hopped out with a coffee travel mug. She had on slightly less makeup than she wore at the bar. Her purple hair was pulled back in a pony-tail, but in such a way as to make the shaved sides of her head less noticeable. She wore a long, colorful sweater down to mid-thigh and black leggings that went down into moon boots. The sweater was cinched with a wide belt. To Dexter, it looked like she had been dressed by Cindy Lauper, Bill Cosby and Napoleon Dynamite. But, all in all, it was professional enough. In fact, Dexter had half expected much worse.

"I hope you haven't been waiting long."

"No, just about five minutes is all."

"Well, I'll get you some keys today."

Dexter unlocked the office door and began showing Gina around. There was a fax machine, a phone, a copier, a computer, and two filing cabinets. For some reason, it had not occurred to Dexter until now that his office was not big enough for the two of them as it was.

"What's that for?" Gina was pointing at a door in the middle of the back wall. It was blocked by Dexter's work station. Like the upstairs, Dexter did not utilize much of the space in his office downstairs. There was in fact a much larger office beyond the main front office Dexter had used exclusively until now.

Together, Dexter and Gina moved the work table out of the way of the door enough to open it. Somehow, the florescent lights still worked back there. Dexter had at one time had big notions about what to do with the space. But, those notions had faded fast and he had kind of forgotten the space was even there.

The space was twice the size of the front office, with a counter and kitchen sink, and a restroom. Dexter had always waited to go pee when he was at the courthouse or would run upstairs. He was a little shocked to realize what he had here, he was also embarrassed that he had forgotten about it. He was not a rich man, how had he forgotten that he owned this? There was an inch of dust and some scraps of paper here and there, and a lot of boxes the previous occupants had left behind that had to be sorted. The carpet was dated, but practically brand new. A good cleaning was what it needed, a new desk for Dexter and a small fridge and a microwave for the counter and they would be set.

"This looks like a job for a couple of middle-aged-mutant-ninja-turtles." Dexter said smiling.

"Oh, no. If you mean who I think you mean, I will need a raise to put up with those two here."

"It will be better than a raise," Dexter assured Gina. "You are going to be their boss. And you are going to work their asses off."

After a few seconds of consideration, Gina realized how much potential enjoyment she could have with this.

A couple of well-placed phone calls and Dexter had Teddy and Pat lined-up to work that afternoon. He took Gina over to the courthouse to show her the routine of checking Dexter's boxes in County Court and District Court and the county attorney's office. Dexter had been dreading the introductions because he was terrible with names, especially the clerks and secretaries in the courthouse. That was probably why so few of them seemed to like him.

Dexter's apprehension soon dissipated as he realized that this was Gina's home town. She already knew everyone in the courthouse. She was even related to a few of them. When the county clerk magistrate came from behind the counter, put her arm around Gina and complimented Dexter on "Finally doing something sensible" by hiring Gina, he realized that Gina was going to be even more of an asset to him than he had imagined.

By lunch, Dexter had trained Gina as much as he ever would. She knew as much as he did about how the office ran. Dexter knew that if things picked-up the way they were expected to, Gina would be growing the management system in ways that he would only be vaguely aware of. Dexter felt better and better about his decision to hire her. To Dexter's relief and surprise, they were also quickly reaching an understanding and rapport. Gina didn't talk that much, but when she did, she said smart, cool things. And, if she thought he talked too much or said stupid, uncool things, she didn't let it show. Gina had a gift, she could be frank without being mean.

Lunch was Dexter's only upper hand. Gina ate at Lee Ho Fook's as much as anyone in town, anyone in town who wasn't Dexter. She was impressed with his private stock of diet Dr. Pepper and the way the waiter asked "lo mein or chicken?" It may have been her hometown Chinese restaurant, it was his dining room.

After eating, Dexter and Gina sat together in her car, listening to the radio and smoked cigarettes until Pat and Teddy showed-up. Pat and Teddy were shown the back room and Gina dispatched Dexter to the store with a shopping list of cleaning supplies. He would also stop by a second-hand furniture store for another desk and more chairs.

When Dexter got back, the front office had been rearranged to suit Gina and Dexter had to admit that it looked much more open and professional. It was also now possible to get into the larger back office from the front.

At the back of the bigger office was a door that lead out to the alley. It was open now, and Gina stood half in and half out of it smoking, while Teddy and Pat sat on the floor next to a stack of boxes discussing Elvis Presley's life as a martial artist.

Dexter stood there, unnoticed for about three minutes, astounded to hear all that Pat and Teddy knew about Elvis Presley and his years of studying martial arts under Ed Parker. If Gina was listening, she wasn't showing it. Dexter had recently heard or read somewhere that to be an "expert" in any subject, you just had to read a book a month on that subject for a year, or spend thirty minutes every day studying that subject. Pat Blocker and Teddy Pickrell were truly experts in the martial arts. And, if their bodies knew half of what their brains knew about karate, they would be very dangerous men. This made Dexter laugh a little.

Dexter handed each of them a bottle of water. "Thanks Dexter." Teddy said. "What you want us to do with these boxes here?"

Dexter looked at the stack of boxes with no recollection at all of ever having seen them. They must have been left by the previous occupants. "Take them out to the dumpster guys."

Gina flicked her cigarette into the alley and stepped inside "I hope it's ok that I had them move these filing cabinets back here. I left the one with the open files up front."

"Sure, it's a smart idea."

"Hey Dexter," Pat cut in. "Do you think you are going to want to paint this place? Cause we could paint this place. We've done a lot of painting for Don Birch. He'll tell you how good we are."

Dexter looked around the room and contemplated the front office too. "Sure, maybe the whole place. But, maybe I need to put some walls up in here first."

"Well, we been trying to get a little work with Bob Schmidt since things fell off with Don. I bet he could fix you up."

"Why did things fall off with Don Birch?"

Pat and Teddy exchanged glances. Teddy spoke, "Well, we really like Mr. Don and he has always been real good to us. But, since that Will Jorgensen has been back, well, he's just kinda taken over everything. He's managing all of Jeff Hays' houses for Linda, Jr. and now he's just kinda moving in on Don's stuff. I think Mrs. Birch and Linda, Jr. and Will are all teaming up on Mr. Don."

"Yeah," Pat broke in, "You would think that Will would be a little more respectful to a man who just killed three fellas."

"If he killed three fellas" Teddy quickly corrected.

"What the hell is that supposed to mean?" Everyone jumped and turned to see Wilbur Pedersen standing in the door between the two offices. He was glaring at Teddy Pickrell.

"What do you mean, Teddy Pickrell, 'IF he killed three fellas?'"

"Hey Mr. Pedersen. Well, you know. He hasn't been found guilty yet. And, the paper said that you dropped one of them murders already." Not wanting to say more, Teddy let it drop.

Wilbur Pedersen did not stop glaring at Teddy as he moved toward Dexter, shoving court documents in Dexter's direction. "Here, it's a new case for you. The complaint and the reports. You and I need to talk about depositions too. I would like to get started next week on them. About half the sheriff's department will be out, training next month. So, the guys we need to depose will either be gone then or covering for those who are gone."

"Sure Will. Gina or I will call over when we finish-up back here in a bit."

"Alright. If I'm not in, just talk to Sally and set them up. And don't forget, Jeremy Wilson is getting sentenced Friday."

Dexter had forgotten all about Jeremy. He hadn't given Jeremy a thought in two weeks. He wondered what Jeremy was up to. He turned to Teddy, who was still following Wilbur out with his eyes. "You think he's still mad at me about that fart?"

"Yes, Teddy. You will probably never be forgiven for it. And, you will almost certainly go to Hell over it too." Dexter said all of this with a grin to let Teddy know he was joking. But, remembering that smell, Dexter wondered if it would send Teddy to Hell. He changed the subject. "So, Teddy, is Jeremy Wilson still working with you guys down at the Burger Hut?"

"Well, he works nights and we work mornings, so we don't work together. But, he's still down there. He's the night-shift manager now." This was pleasantly surprising news to Dexter.   Dexter and the boys moved the new furniture in when it arrived from the used furniture store. When that was done, he told Gina to call Sally about setting up those depositions. Then, Dexter headed over to the probation office. He was anxious to see what they would be recommending for Jeremy at sentencing.

Dexter felt good about Jeremy's sentencing hearing when it came around. Jeremy's parents were there. Jeremy was in a new pair of slacks, dress shoes, a blue button-down shirt and a belt. His face was fuller than it had been in a long time and his eyes almost had a light in them again. His hair was neatly trimmed, and he looked his age, not older, for a change.

The probation office had not exactly made a recommendation to the Judge, but rather expressed a willingness to continue to work with Jeremy, should the Judge give him another opportunity at probation.

Dexter felt confident. Jeremy was nervous, so were his parents. Dexter tried to convince them everything would be alright, but they just wouldn't let themselves.

The Judge came in and took his seat and everyone else sat. Wilbur Pedersen was unmoved by everything Jeremy had done to turn his life around over the past several weeks. He pointed out that this was now Jeremy's fourth probation violation. He argued that at some point, to ensure the integrity of the Court, the meaning of probation and the meaning of punishment, Jeremy Wilson's probation had to be revoked and he had to be sentenced to a term of incarceration.

Dexter stood confidently. He recited all the positive things Jeremy had done over the last several weeks. He had not missed a single probation appointment. He had not missed a single counseling session. He had attended at least three AA meetings a week, every week. He was now the assistant manager at Burger Hut and he had paid all but three hundred dollars of his restitution.

Then it was Jeremy's turn to speak. "Your Honor, I just want to thank you for all the opportunities you have already given me. I want to thank my parents for always supporting me and never giving up on me. And, I want to apologize for all the time I have wasted of the Court, the State, and the probation office. That's all I have to say sir."

Judge Ostergart folded his hands on his bench in front of him. He took a deep breathe, let it out and began to speak. "Mr. Wilson, in sentencing you, I have considered your age, your education, your social and cultural background. I have considered your criminal history, your history of law abiding conduct. I have considered the nature of the offense, I have considered the motivation for the offense, and I have considered the fact that there was no violence involved in the offense.

"I appreciate the efforts you have made over the last several weeks and I have factored them into my decision.

But, to place you on probation yet again, at this point, would promote disrespect for the law, for this Court and for the entire criminal justice system. It is therefore the order of the Court that your probation be revoked and that you be sentenced to the Nebraska Department of Corrections for a term of incarceration not to exceed forty-two months but not to be less than twenty-one months. The probation office report shows that from the time of your arrest until now, including all the sanctions in your probation and all the arrests for probation violations, you have served fifty-three days. I give you credit for those fifty-three days against that sentence that I have now imposed. It is so ordered. You are remanded to the custody of the deputies for imposition of the sentence."

Dexter was stunned. He had not seen that coming. He was the only one. He turned to Jeremy. "I'm sorry man. I really thought you had done well enough lately to earn another shot."

"No Dexter. It's time. I appreciate all you tried to do for me. This is all on me. So, what am I looking at?"

Dexter bent over his notes and ran some figures. "At forty-two months, you jam in twenty-one months. Subtract the fifty-three days credit and you have about nineteen months to jam. That means you could be paroled in eleven or thirteen months."

"Year, year and a half. I can do that."

The deputy led Jeremy toward the back door of the courtroom. His parents were there. His mother was crying. The deputy let them hug, then cuffed Jeremy's hands in front of him and lead him away.

****

Dexter skulked back to the office. He thought that maybe he should have expected this after all. Everyone else had. Maybe he was just riding too high from his successes in the Don Birch case. The more he thought about it, the more he started to realize this was the only thing that could have happened. He also realized that it could have been worse.

He also thought that with the new contract, he would get more serious cases than he was accustomed to. Having clients go to prison would become much more frequent for him. He needed to get used to that fact.

The distraction Dexter needed from Jeremy Wilson met him at the front door of his office. Gina was on the phone with someone and trying to deal with a UPS guy at the same time. Dexter also heard a commotion of some sort in the back office. Then, the other line started to ring, and Dexter finally noticed a little guy who looked to be in his fifties sitting in a chair. He had shoulder length hair and a bewildered look on his face.

"Dexter Smith?"

"Yes."

"Would you sign here sir?"

Dexter signed, and the UPS guy handed him a box and walked out. Gina was on the second phone line now, so, already forgetting the little guy, Dexter walked into the back office to find Bob Schmidt with a tape measurer in his hand, barking numbers to Teddy who was holding a clipboard. Pat was there too, trying to look relevant.

"What's going on?" Dexter asked, not as irritated as confused.

Bob Schmidt looked a little confused that Dexter wasn't expecting him to be there. "Oh, the boys here told me you wanted to put some walls up back here, and Gina and I were trying to figure out where they should go."

Dexter thanked Bob for getting right on the project but explained that he wasn't quite ready to get started. He also had to explain to Bob that while Dexter was representing Mildred Pedersen for assaulting Bob, Dexter couldn't hire Bob to do any work. It might look like a bribe or like Dexter could influence Bob where the case was concerned. "But, as soon as we get this case behind us, I will be glad to have you come in and take a crack at this."

"I hadn't thought of that. I guess we need to get that taken care of first. But, while I'm here, you sure you don't want to just quick-walk through this and show me what you want?"

"Better not Bob. Besides, I'm sure you and Gina have it all worked out. As soon as Mrs. Pedersen's case is out of the way, we will get right on this."

With Bob and the boys out of the office, Dexter turned his attention back to Gina and the little fella in the front office.

"Dexter, this is Mr. Sanders, that new case Mr. Pedersen brought over the other day. Here is the file." Dexter nodded and smiled at Tom Sanders as he took the file and flipped it open. Dexter knitted his eyebrows and his smile vanished as he saw that this nice little man was charged with three counts of Terroristic Threats, one count of Use of a Firearm to Commit a Felony, and a count of Discharging a Firearm in an Occupied Dwelling.

Dexter thumbed quickly through the several pages of police reports to see that two pages were vital data on the involved parties, two were copies of hand-written statements, and the rest, the bulk of the report, was the police narrative of the alleged incident.

Dexter looked up and smiled again at Mr. Sanders. "Tom, why don't you give me a couple of minutes to review this and then I will have Gina send you back." Dexter walked into the back office and sat at his new, used desk and began reading.

On the above time and date, the above-named deputy was on duty, in a marked patrol vehicle, wearing a uniform and displaying the badge of office. This deputy proceeded to the above listed address in reference to a 911 call by the sole owner and occupant of that residence, Thomas Sanders, who called 911 to report the theft of a six-pound, maple cured, spiral cut, Virginia ham.

Upon arrival at the residence, this deputy made contact with Mr. Sanders, who informed me that just prior to his calling 911, Bill Fitzsimons had run out of the back door of Mr. Sanders' residence and grabbed the ham off the kitchen counter on his way out the back door. Mr. Sanders went on to explain that he had just won the ham in a raffle at Johnson's Market and was intending to take it to a family reunion that following weekend.

Bill Fitzsimons is known to this deputy through prior contacts and I asked Mr. Sanders how he knew Mr. Fitzsimons and how Mr. Fitzsimons came to be in Mr. Sanders' home. Sanders informed me that he and Mr. Fitzsimons were life-long friends and that Fitzsimons was in the home when Sanders returned home from work this day. I asked Sanders if he was sure it was Fitzsimons and he answered in the affirmative and then showed me a wallet that contained the driver's license of William Fitzsimons as well as Mr. Fitzsimons' EBT card. I asked Mr. Sanders where he had found these items and he told me they were in the back pocket of the pants he found in the bedroom floor. This surprised me somewhat, so I then asked Sanders what Fitzsimons was wearing when he left with the ham and Sanders answered "nothing."

I asked Sanders why Fitzsimons would run out of the house naked and Sanders replied, "Because I chased him the hell out of here." I then asked for clarification. He replied that I would have to ask Cheryl why Fitzsimons was naked. I asked who "Cheryl" was and was told that Cheryl is Cheryl Carp, the girlfriend of Sanders. Sanders then quickly corrected himself saying that she was probably now his ex-girlfriend. Sanders went on to explain that when he got home he found Cheryl and Bill together in his bed and that he proceeded to chase Bill out of the house with his 380 Hi-Point pistol. I asked if there were any other witnesses to all of this and Sanders answered "Yes, Rhonda was here too." This deputy then asked more questions and ascertained that "Rhonda" was the younger cousin of Sanders and that she was also naked and in his bed along with Bill and Cheryl.

This deputy next proceeded to the address known to me to be that of William Fitzsimons. I found Fitzsimons on the steps of his trailer house talking with his neighbor, Wendel "Harley" Parker. As I pulled up, Parker went back to his own trailer. I noticed that Fitzsimons was wearing only a bathrobe and was eating what appeared to be a sandwich of maple cured ham.

I asked Fitzsimons if he had any idea why I was there, and he answered, "For the ham." I told him yes and asked him why he took the ham. He responded by saying "I guess screwing two women at once and then getting shot at just makes me hungry."

Mr. Fitzsimons then told me the same story about what had happened as Mr. Sanders had told, with the addition of the information that Sanders had fired his pistol, which Sanders had not mentioned. I asked Fitzsimons if he thought he had permission to be in Mr. Sanders' home and he told me that he knew he did not have permission to be there. I cited him for first degree trespassing and theft of the ham. He complained that he should not be charged because he was shot at. I told Fitzsimons that Sanders was going to be arrested for that and Mr. Fitzsimons asked me not to do that and said that it was his fault and that he did not want to press charges against Mr. Sanders. I informed him that it was not up to him, but the County Attorney to press charges and left the residence.

I then made contact with Cheryl Carp. Ms. Carp confirmed everything that had been told to me by the others, I cited her for trespassing and she too asked that Mr. Sanders not be arrested.

Upon contact with Rhonda Sanders, Ms. Sanders refused to provide a statement and denied any knowledge of the events. I cited her for trespassing. This officer then returned to the residence of Thomas Sanders. I asked him if he had in fact fired his gun while chasing the others out of the home. He admitted that he had. I told him he was under arrest for Terroristic Threats, Use of a Firearm to Commit a Felony, and Discharging a Firearm in an Occupied Dwelling. I took him into custody without incident.

Dexter dropped the report back into the file, placed his elbows on the desk and his head in his hands. "Holy shit" is all he could say. It came out more as a gasp. Jeremy Wilson's sentencing hearing had been forever pushed from his mind.

13

Dexter sat across from Gina at The Pawnee Club. They had started a routine of alternating lunch between The Pawnee Club and Lee Ho Fooks. "He's such a nice little guy. It's crazy." Dexter complained.

"I know. The whole town has been talking about this. You know he's a war hero, right?'

"What?" Dexter had not known this about his newest client.

"Yeah, he fought in the Granada Invasion. The only person from here who fought there. If it hadn't been for him, we wouldn't have had a parade. Well, they wouldn't have had a parade. I wasn't born yet."

Dexter had to scan the look on Gina's face to make sure she was being serious. Was he now being told that this guy was a war hero simply because he was the only person in the town to participate in the Grenada Invasion and thus the only reason the town could have a parade? He really wanted to have Gina elaborate, but decided not to. Maybe he could ask Sam about it sometime.

"So, yeah, everyone is real upset with Bill Fitzsimons and Cheryl. Rhonda is probably going to move to Omaha, her family is so mad at her. I don't think Mr. Pedersen or the Judge will want to go too hard on Tom. I think you'll get a good deal offered to you pretty quick."

"Well, I hope you're right about getting a quick deal. Especially considering the circumstances, I think anyone would have done the same thing. Maybe I should look into an insanity defense, just in case we aren't offered anything. That had to be a shock to the system. Caught his best friend, his girlfriend, and his cousin all together like that. In his own bed."

"And then one of them stole his ham." They looked seriously at each other and nodded in agreement.

After eating, Dexter asked Gina "Well, what all do you have planned for me, in the near future?"

"Well, you have an appointment with Mildred Pedersen Monday morning. You have two bankruptcy consultations on Tuesday. "

"Wait, I don't do bankruptcy work. I never have done them. I don't know how."

"Don't worry. I've helped with a couple. We just need to get the software, I will do the forms online. They are very clerical. I do them, you sign off on them, we file them, and once a month you go over to federal court and do the hearings. They take about five minutes each. Tom McWilliams can take you along with him sometime and show you how they're done."

"Well, I'll give them a try. What else have you planned for me?"

"Well, Don Birch canceled his appointment for Monday, his wife has to go somewhere out of town, so they rescheduled."

"Don can't come in by himself? He's my client. I would really like to spend a little time with just him."

"Ha, good luck with that. Not much she lets him do without her. She's always afraid he'll embarrass her. He lives with that woman for forty-five years without ever once complaining in the slightest and then goes off and kills three other people?"

"You're starting to sound like Teddy, you don't think Don did it either? He confessed for Christ-sake."

"Yeah, well a lot of people think it's an odd situation."

"Yeah, he made all three of his daughters widows because he thought he was going to die, then he found out he wasn't. That is a pretty odd situation."

"No, it's odd that he killed Jeff. He loved Jeff like a son. It's odd that Linda Jr. and Will Jorgensen are spending so much time together, and some say they were seeing a lot of each other before Jeff was killed. It is odd that Don Birch's wife and daughters act like he has died already or still may, even though the doctors say he won't."

Dexter let this soak in. He had felt uneasy about something for a while too but had no idea what. Gina was now showing him what the rest of the town, the people who knew the Birch family, thought about the whole mess.

"OK Gina, call Don when we get back to the office and tell him I need to talk to him on Monday, without his wife, and I will still meet with them both later in the week. What else do I have next week?"

"The caseworker in the Parker Juvenile case called to say she has set-up a team meeting next week. Sounds like things aren't going well, so you really need to be there. She is going to drop off a progress report sometime before the meeting."

"OK, I'll need to look at that as soon as it comes in and hopefully I can have a meeting with Gracie June and Harley before the team meeting. What about depositions in Don's cases?"

"Those start two weeks from yesterday."

"How are we fixed for office supplies now?"

"We're pretty good for now. I'll let you know when we need stuff. Speaking of, what was in the UPS box this morning?"

"Oh, just a couple of suits I got off eBay."

"What? You buy suits online? You don't even get to try them on."

"Well, yeah. I mean, look at it this way. Some guy goes out and buys a five-hundred-dollar suit for his cousin's wedding or his grandma's funeral. Hell, even doctors and bankers wear polos and khakis these days, so that suit hangs in his closet for a couple of years. He goes on some crash diet or something and loses weight, or he gains more weight and he doesn't need the suit anymore. He sells it on eBay for fifty to one-hundred-dollars, just to get something out of it. I buy it for that price, and even if I have to get it altered, I get a five-hundred-dollar suit for under a hundred bucks, and it's only been worn once."

"Wow, so you don't just wear Dickies?"

"I mostly wear Dickies. They are just khakis after all. They last forever, so not only do I save money on pants, I have to watch my weight, so I don't outgrow them."

Gina didn't know what to say. No one in town who knew Dexter Smith had ever had a really bad thing to say about him. But, since he had shown up in town and hung his shingle, everyone thought he was a little odd. Gina knew she had no room to judge, it had never been in her nature anyway. Where Dexter was concerned, she had never really thought much of him one way or another, except for the androgyny thing. She was now finding him to be kind of interesting. She was starting to think working for him might be amusing.

It took some doing, but that afternoon Gina convinced Don and Linda Birch that Don was quite capable of meeting with his lawyer all by himself. Gina could be firm with people in a way Dexter could not. Linda had started off by refusing to allow the meeting. Gina asked Linda pointedly to explain why it was a problem which seemed to put Linda on the defensive and make her very nervous.

Dexter and Gina discussed all of this while Dexter stood on a chair in the middle of the front office in one of his newish suits while Gina pinned and marked it for alterations. "So," Dexter puzzled "You seriously think there is more to Don's case than what we all know?"

"Yes, and not just me. Most of the women in town who know Linda Birch well think something is up. That includes all the women in the County Attorney's Office.

They told me the other day that Wilbur Pedersen has forbidden them to talk about it in the office anymore."

Dexter was trying to absorb all of this when the phone rang. Gina had been conveying all of this to Dexter through a mouth full of pins. Before reaching for the phone, Gina grabbed Dexter's hand, turned it palm up and spat the pins into it before grabbing the receiver and speaking in her clearest, most professional voice.

"Yes, he is in. I will see if he is available.

"It's the lawyer from the Attorney General's Office about Mildred Pedersen's case. He sounds upset. Do you want to talk to him?"

"Sure, if you can keep working on this while I talk." Gina took the pins from his hand and replaced them with the receiver.

"Dexter Smith here."

"Smith, what the hell are you trying to pull out there? You want to explain yourself to me, or should I let you and the Counsel for Discipline work it out?"

"Good afternoon to you too, and just what in the hell are you talking about, may I ask?" Dexter was usually good natured to the point of being timid, but when he was confronted out of the blue like this, he reacted in kind.

"I'm talking about this Mildred Pedersen case and the conversation I just had with her victim. Do you deny telling him that you would hire him to remodel your office if this case went away?"

Dexter didn't know whether to laugh or cry. It would probably depend on how this deputy AG responded to the explanation he was about to give. Dexter let out a mild chuckle to try to change the tone "Look, I had a couple of guys who do odd jobs around town help me move some furniture the other day. They and my assistant and I got to talking about some things that could be done to the office in the near future. The next thing I know, I come back from court this morning and the two guys are in my office with

Bob Schmidt measuring the place. They were just trying to drum up some business for Bob, so he would hire them to help out."

"And you told Bob Schmidt that if he called me and made this case go away, you would let him do this work for you."

"No," Dexter said, starting to get irritated again. "I told him it was a conflict and explained how it would look. And I told him that when the case was over AND when I was ready to do the work, I would probably have him do the work. And, the reason I will probably have him do the work is because I don't know anyone around here who would do the job better. Look, it's a misdemeanor case, I have a fifteen-hundred-dollar retainer to do it. I'm not risking my practice for that."

"What about the new contract Mrs. Pedersen's son helped you land with the county? That doesn't figure into all of this?"

"Hell no. No." Dexter was now starting to get nervous. "I got that contract because no one else wanted it. The contract is the reason I need to redo my office. This is a small town. I am one of only a few lawyers in the area. Bob Schmidt is one of only a few carpenters around here. This stuff just happens."

Though still irritated, the deputy AG seemed to believe Dexter and backed off a little. "Well, I guess this makes sense, at least enough to convince the Counsel for Discipline if I did pursue this further.

"So, look. You guys are short a judge. I don't want to drive all the way out there, and now my main witness is back-peddling on me, and he was never keen on cooperating to begin with. But I don't like it one bit. People like the Pedersens can't just run small towns like their own fiefdoms. But, you tell Mildred Pedersen that if she does twenty hours of community service at a hospital or nursing home and agrees to pay court costs, I will dismiss the case."

Dexter handed the receiver back to Gina, feeling like maybe he led a charmed life. He just wished he could get a couple of personal injury cases while he was on this hot streak.

Mildred Pedersen was elated come Monday morning with the news Dexter gave her. So much so, she probably exonerated him for his part in the funeral fiasco. "Oh, Dexter. Thank you so much. I really don't know how to thank you. And, I have already agreed to take over playing piano at the nursing home worship service, so finding a few more things to do around there will be no problem at all for my community service."

She said all of this making her way to the outer office and the door when she stopped and turned to Gina and then back to Dexter. "Maybe I could talk Gina into giving a painting class at the nursing home, and I could be her assistant." She turned back to Gina, smiling and Gina forced a reciprocal smile.

"Oh, Gina, tell Bernice that I have her casserole dish from the funeral lunch at my house. I don't know how it ended up in my car."

"I will tell her."

"Goodbye Dexter, and thank you again so much."

As soon as Mrs. Pedersen was out the door and headed down the sidewalk Dexter turned to Gina. "Who the hell is Bernice?"

"My grandmother, asshole. She and Mrs. Pedersen are very close friends, and both are very active in our church."

"And the painting class? You are just full of hidden talents."

"Hidden? Everyone knows about my painting. And, I am a certified Bob Ross landscape instructor. Mrs. Pedersen and my grandmother and another friend of theirs all pitched in and sent me to Florida as a high school graduation present to take the instructors' class."

"I just never would have guessed that the two of you would be so close."

"It's a small town. The woman was my Sunday school teacher and my piano teacher. The woman is my grandmother's best friend. Everyone knows everyone around here to some degree whether they want to admit it or not."

Gina handed Dexter the social worker's report on the Parker family. It was not good. Gracie June was sleeping too much, Harley could not get daycare assistance while he was at work because he was not the parent. The baby was not putting on weight and was diagnosed with failure to thrive, probably due to Gracie June not getting up to feed her. Harley is irritable and exhausted from trying to care for the child and working. Gracie June has a bruise on her left cheek that she cannot or will not account for. "Well," Dexter muttered to himself as he threw the report back on Gina's desk, "That's just frigging great."

Don Birch was right on time for his appointment. He was cheerful and pleasant, as usual, but a little nervous.

"Afternoon Dexter." Don said as Gina showed him to his seat in Dexter's new office. Don looked around admiring the new space. Nothing really had been done with it, but there was potential.

"You got a nice, big space back here. Real nice, got new carpet I see."

"Well, actually, this is pretty old carpet. It's just never seen the light of day back here Don. I kept this closed-up. I never really needed it until recently when I got busy and had to hire Gina."

"Well, I'm guessing I have something to do with that uptick in business." Don looked mildly embarrassed when he said this.

"Not at all. A lot of things are changing around town and the courthouse, little by little. But, I'm glad we have a chance to talk today, just the two of us. I don't always feel like I can talk candidly to you, or you to me, when your wife is here."

"Yeah, she wasn't too happy about not being here. She likes being in control. Doesn't trust me to say the right things and what not."

"What do you mean 'right' things Don? I'm your lawyer, you can speak freely with me. Maybe more freely with me than your wife even. Nothing you say can leave this room. Besides, your confession is thrown out, but that doesn't mean we forget about it, pretend you never said what you already said."

"Yeah, I know, and even if there were other things I told you, they would stay between us, right?"

"Exactly. I can't put on evidence at trial, including testimony from a witness that I know is false, based on what you told me. And, I can't give advice on an on-going crime. But, anything you tell me Don, stays between us, unless you try to get me to violate one of those rules. That rule holds truer right now, because your wife is not here. It really is just the two of us. Attorney/client."

Don got a funny look on his face and looked down at his boot without talking for what seemed like a long time. Given all the rumors starting to circulate around town, Dexter had realized that he would need to have a frank conversation with Don about what was really going on. Dexter just didn't know how to start that conversation. It was now occurring to Dexter that the conversation had just begun.

"So, Don. Now that it is just you and me here, what do your daughters think of all of this? I mean, how are things now between you and them?"

Don laughed nervously and finally looked up from his boot. "Well Dexter, I don't know. Marcia has all her medical problems and doctor's appointments, so I don't ever see much of her. But she doesn't seem mad.

"Debra and I were always the closest. I think she understands how dangerous Scott could be. He was a good man and a hard worker when he was sober. But when he started getting into drugs and alcohol, well, he was just dangerous, that's all.

"But, things are different between me and Debra too. She still loves me. She tells me that every time she sees me. But. I don't know. She does her own thing now and doesn't see much of any of us. I am worried about her.

"Linda Jr. She and her mom are thick and always have been. And now with that Will Jorgensen around, the three of them just act like I don't even exist sometimes or I'm feeble minded or something. Jeff was a good boy. He was a hard worker. He just wasn't good enough for my wife, and once Jorgensen came back around, Jeff wasn't good enough for Linda Jr. either. I think he was too much like me for their liking."

Don looked back down at his boot now. Dexter wanted to ask Don why he would kill Jeff if that's how he felt. But Dexter knew he wouldn't get a good answer. Don probably didn't have a good answer to give, unless it was an answer he wasn't ready to share with Dexter. Dexter was going to have to coax this out of Don over time, he decided to let it go for the time being. Don sensed this and was relieved.

"So, Don. We have these depositions coming up. This Sanchez fella who rents from you, what do you know about him?"

"To start with, I don't think his name is Sanchez. And, I don't think he's around anymore. His family was out of that house when I got out of jail and I don't know where they are now."

"Do you think, maybe, he was not here legally?"

"I can't say for sure, but that's what I figured."

"Ok, well that's kinda good, and kinda bad. You see, that is one less thing to link you to Roy's murder. But, Sanchez said he saw your truck leaving Roy's office about the same time Joe Friesen heard the shot over at Jeff's house."

"Well, I couldn't be in two places at once. Joe Friesen is crazy. And deaf as a post to boot."

"Well, that is an argument for the state to make, not us. We don't want to discredit a possible alibi. Of course, without Sanchez to testify about a time, Friesen won't be much of an alibi."

"So, are we trying to pin all this on someone else now?"

"No, we just show that maybe it wasn't you."

"But, then, they look for someone else."

"Probably not. They can't use your confession, but they won't forget it either. But even if they do try to pin it on someone else, that isn't for us to consider."

"I just don't want to stir anything up and draw anyone else into all this."

Dexter felt like this was drifting back naturally to that frank conversation they needed to have. "Don, is there something you aren't telling me about all of this that you should?"

"No. Dexter, I think I need to be going. I don't like thinking about all of this for too long. Can we pick it up later this week?"

"Sure Don."

Dexter couldn't decide if the meeting had gone well or not. Things were not at all what they seemed. Donald Birch was hiding something, but not well. Dexter had hoped the conversation would have convinced him that all the speculation in town about Donald Birch was nonsense. It had not. So, could Dexter get to the bottom of everything? Would he want to get to the bottom of everything?

Dexter needed to mull all this over and spend some quality time with Sam Hagan. "Gina, are you really going to need me here to meet with those bankruptcy clients?"

"I can't imagine why I would."

"Well, I'm going down to spend a little quality time with your uncle."

"Hey, I'm sure you've done at least three hours of work in the five hours you've been here today. You've earned the rest of the day off."

"Thanks, smartass."

14

Sam had done most of his bar prep and was now cutting lemons up just as Dexter was finishing he tale of woe. "So, I usually talk to Tom McWilliams about this kind of thing, but it is getting a little too close to the Musgrave probate case. I shouldn't be discussing my client's case at all. But, hell, I don't see how I can violate the attorney/client communication when Don won't communicate with me. What do I do?"

"How the hell should I know? I'm sorry, but what's gotten into you? This guy is going to give you the run around and play a game that only he can lose. Seems to me the cops have done a pretty good job of sewing this case up for the prosecution in spite of the confession issue. Now, your client could do something to help himself, and you, but he won't. I don't know Dex. You have your head in the game. You are doing all you need to, all you can do. I don't know what more you want. This isn't a movie. You can't expect everything to fall neatly into place with a happy ending.

"But, I can tell you, Linda Jr. and Will Jorgensen are up to no good. They had Don in here for lunch today, I guess before he went to meet with you. And, I don't know what they were saying to him, but they were talking to him like a dog."

Dexter raised his eyebrows, not really knowing what to say.

"Well, depositions start soon. Those should shed a whole new light on things."

"I hope those help, but my money says unless you or someone starts taking a closer look at his wife and daughters, and Will Jorgensen, no one will ever get to the bottom of any of this. God knows your client isn't going to help, even if it would save his own neck. He's letting all of this happen, so

I don't feel bad for him. Even if he didn't kill those three, he has something to do with it. I just don't like the rest of them getting away with anything."

"Wow, I never knew you to be a conspiracy theorist Sam."

"Laugh now smartass but mark my words. There is a lot more to this, just wait."

Dexter passed the rest of the night in relative quiet, opting to eat a burger there at the bar for dinner. When Pat and Teddy came in, he told them that it would probably be alright for them and Bob Schmidt to start working on the new office.

Dexter dragged into the office the next morning about half an hour after Gina had opened. He wasn't hungover or anything, he was just starting to slip back into his old slothful habits. "Morning Gina, what's on today's schedule?"

"Well, Wilbur Pedersen just called, and he wants to meet you and the sheriff at 9:30. And, Harley and Gracie June are coming in after lunch. And, a visiting judge will be in County Court this afternoon, so they want to have Tom Sanders' preliminary hearing at 3."

"What does Wilbur want?"

"He just said it was about Don Birch. He wouldn't get more specific."

After a couple of cups of coffee and a cigarette in the alley, Dexter made his way over to the courthouse and Wilbur's office. He was met by Wilbur's staff with their usual warmth "He says you can go right in," was exactly everything the one who sat in front said to him. He was going to make Gina draw up a seating chart of everyone in the courthouse, so he could learn these women's names.

Wilbur stopped talking in midsentence and looked up at Dexter when he came into the office. Sheriff Coffee and

Chief Deputy Bob Anderson turned in their seats to see him. "OK. Grab a seat Dexter. Want some coffee?"

"No thanks, I just had some."

Dexter sat on the couch as Wilbur came around from his desk to join him and the other two turned their chairs to join in.

"Look, I have to disclose any exculpatory evidence to you that we uncover. So, what the hell have you heard about Linda Hays and Will Jorgensen?"

"Just a lot of rumors and conspiracy theories."

"Well that is what we are getting too. So, Bob here has been looking into things. Seems those two were seen together, along with her mother, down at the bowling alley quite a bit for a few weeks leading up to these murders. Now, on the night of the murders, it was just Will and Linda, Jr. Then mom showed up and Will left, then Linda, Jr. left and then came back, and about half an hour later all this crap hit the fan. So, what does your client tell you about all this?"

"You know I couldn't tell you if he had told me something, unless he wanted me to. Not that he has told me anything, which is something I probably also shouldn't be telling you."

Bod Anderson leaned forward unable to contain what he was busting to say. "Look Smith, we may all be on the same side here, trying to help your client out, so don't blow smoke up our asses."

"Look, my client hasn't told me anything about any of this. And I don't know why he wouldn't if there's anything to all the rumors going around. Besides, if he did confess to something he didn't do and now he comes in and gives you a different story; you have him on the hook for aiding and abetting or some conspiracy theory. You are just getting a confession back in that you can use to prosecute him all over again."

"I would look favorably on anything Don wanted to straighten out at this point," Wilbur assured Dexter. "Plus,

Dennis and Bob here are worried about your client's safety more than anything at this point."

Sheriff Coffee spoke now for the first time. "Dexter, if these three girls are involved in killing their husbands, who's to say their mother won't be able to do the same with hers? And let's face it, if the girls are involved, mother is involved. Look, this all started with everyone thinking that Don Birch was going to die soon. Were they looking for a way to get rid of all their men at once? We want to talk to Don, not just to get to the bottom of the other murders, but to make sure he doesn't end up a fourth victim."

"Let me put it another way." Wilbur broke back in, "We let your client out on an OR bond because of a medical condition he doesn't have. I am going to set a hearing next week asking the Judge to reinstate the old bond."

"You are going to throw my client back in jail for something you are now saying he probably didn't do? Just to sweat the truth out of him? Wow, for cops and prosecutors, I always thought you guys were pretty fair when it counted."

"We are throwing him back in jail because he is charged with two counts of murder. And, if he isn't guilty, then he could be in danger himself. Putting him in jail keeps him safe."

"Oh, so you are just being paternalistic. That's not so bad. You three are real princes. OK. I'll talk to my client about all of this and get back to you, if he lets me." Dexter left. He knew that Wilbur and the sheriff were right. It was looking less and less likely that Don was a murderer, at least not one who worked alone. But, it was obvious that Don knew who did kill those other three men and that he was covering for them. Dexter had also wondered a few times in the back of his mind if the bond issue was ever going to come back up. When he got back to the office, Dexter called Don to break the news to him.

Of course, Mrs. Birch answered the phone and Dexter had a hell of a time trying to get her to put Don on the phone. So, finally he just told her about the bond hearing. They agreed that it could be discussed further at the appointment the Birches had in a couple of days. Dexter did make it a point to ask that Don come in about half an hour ahead of Mrs. Birch. She didn't like the sound of that at all. "Mr. Smith. My husband has repeatedly told you that I may be at all of his appointments and that I am to know everything that goes on in his case."

"Yes, Mrs. Birch. I am aware of that. But you have to understand that I have some say in this as well. I don't mean to be pushy or rude but there are just times when I need to visit alone with my client. After all, when these matters go to trial, you won't be allowed to sit at the defense table with us. Your husband and I need to have a strong rapport when that time comes."

Dexter finally made her understand and agree that her husband would come to the next appointment about thirty minutes ahead of her.

At a quarter till noon, Bob Schmidt showed up with the middle-aged mutant ninja turtles. Gina lead them back to Dexter's office and announced them. "I told Bob and the guys that they could come in and do what they needed to while you were at lunch today."

Bob had some ideas about the back room that he shared with Dexter. They were good ideas, practical and simple. He promised Dexter he would have a close estimate of the cost by early afternoon, as soon as he got the measurements he needed.

Dexter and Gina went to The Pawnee Club for lunch. It was a Lee Ho Fook's day, but Dexter needed a drink. He had a coffee mug of Jack Daniels with his cheeseburger. When he wanted a refill after he had finished eating, Sam looked to Gina for approval first. She nodded approval. The worst of his day was probably over. He didn't need to be too sober to meet with Harley and Gracie June, and he would be fine by the preliminary hearing that afternoon.

By the time they were finished eating and visiting and had had a couple of cigarettes each, it was after one. They got back to the office to find Bob and the boys still there and Harley and Gracie June waiting for their appointment. It was fifteen minutes before the appointment. Dexter and Gina had no way of knowing how long they had been there, waiting. What they were sure of was the nervous tension in the room. Harley looked exhausted and haggard. He had obviously lost weight since the last time Dexter had seen him. He also looked ready to throttle Pat and Teddy. Pat and Teddy did not notice this, they only noticed Gracie June, who was doing her best to wring every ounce of attention from those two. Bob Schmidt was nervous as hell. They were there on his account and he wanted to get the hell out of there with them as soon as possible. But, the more he hurried his measuring to get done, the more trouble he had with it. He wasn't getting any help from his assistants either. "Well, shoot. Dexter. I thought I would have this done by now. We'll get out of here and I can come back later, on my own, and finish up. Come on boys."

Gina finally took charge. She assumed herself between Gracie June and the boys and ushered Gracie June and her brother to Dexter's office. Bob grabbed the boys by the collars and dragged them out the front door.

Dexter settled in behind his desk with the social worker's report in his hand. Gracie June's client file was under it, opened on the desk. Dexter looked first at Gracie June, all childlike smiles for no other reason than she was getting attention, first from Pat and Teddy and now from Dexter. This was all about her. Harley, who was referred to as Wendel in the report, just looked tired and angry. But, mostly tired. Life was wearing on him hard.

"Have you gone over this report with the case worker yet?" Dexter asked Harley.

"Yeah," was Harley's reply, answering for both of them. "They put June Grace in respite care for now and the case worker went over it with us then. I think it's over Mr. Smith. We can't drag it out forever. Gracie can't take care of the baby without me, and I have to have a job with a baby around." Harley looked down at the floor, he was about to cry. Gracie June looked at him with a sympathetic little smile on her face. She put her arm around him and her head on his shoulder.

Dexter went over the procedure with them for relinquishing parental rights. He took his time to make sure Gracie June understood that it was forever and that it could not be undone. She seemed to understand all of it pretty well. She had no attention span to stay sad about it for very long and she was tired of playing at being a mom. Dexter called the case worker. It was agreed the team meeting set later in the week would now be a meeting where by Gracie June would start filling out paper work to relinquish her parental rights to June Grace. There was no need for anyone but the case worker, Gracie June, and Dexter to be there. The case worker would call off everyone else and let them know what was going on.

Dexter hung-up the phone, nodded a sad smile at Harley and watched the two get up and walk out of his office.

****

Twenty minutes later, Gina stuck her head into Dexter's office "It's Phil Taft on the phone for you."

Dexter had not seen Phil since the funeral. They had no cases together at the moment. Dexter rarely dealt with Phil at all. He wondered what this was about. "Hey Phil."

"Hey Dex. Do you know if they ever got that smell out of the church?"

"I have not heard, but I could ask around for you. Wilbur Pedersen would know."

"Well, I need to talk to Wilbur after I talk to you. I just got a call from Linda Birch. She wants to hire me to represent her husband." Well, thought Dexter. That had not taken her long at all. This lady really didn't want her husband talking to anyone without her present. Was she a complete control freak, or was she really trying to hide something?

"So, Dexter, I'm not poaching here. She called me. I told her I would need a twenty-thousand-dollar retainer to start, and she said they had plenty of real estate to put up as collateral and that they were going to start liquidating some of the real estate pretty soon."

"You aren't hurting my feelings any. But I am surprised that they are going to sell off some of their property."

"Well, I didn't think you would mind too much. Any time a client wants to change lawyers in mid case, I figure it is the client not wanting to face the hard truth of things."

"I think Linda Birch is worried about the truth alright. I will tell Gina to send you the file as soon as we get your appearance of counsel. I'm court appointed, so you aren't hurting my feelings any by taking this case. And, I don't care if you take my work product. I think there may be a hearing next week, so talk to Wilbur about that and you can pick the file up when you come into town for that hearing."

"Thanks Dexter, I should have asked for a hundred-thousand. Sometimes it's easier to scare them off with a big number than to take a well-paying case that's a pain in the ass."

"It's your pain in the ass now Phil. I'll be here to help if you need anything."

"Thanks Dexter."

Dexter went over to the courthouse a little early for Tom Sanders' preliminary hearing to find Wilbur. He was outside of the County Court room. "You talk to Phil Taft yet Will?"

"I did."

"And?"

"And the church still smells like Satin's own asshole."

"Is that all you have to say about the call?"

"You know what I know, we'll see what happens."

"Well, what about Tom Sanders?"

"Have him plead to third degree assault, threatening in a menacing manner on Cheryl Carp, and I will dismiss the other counts."

"Wow, are you giving him the war hero special? Going to blame this on the PTSD from Granada?"

"I have three of the worst victims possible if he decides he wants a jury. Two of them are begging me to drop the whole thing and the third denies it happened. I will ask for a fine and the day he already spent in jail before he bonded out."

"Wow, I've been on quite the winning streak lately."

"Yeah, well. We all have those streaks, they always come to an end."

Tom was all for the plea offer, the visiting judge was not. But, Wilbur Pedersen was an experienced prosecutor whose judgement was well respected. The judge went along with the agreement but gave Tom Sanders a good dressing down from the bench and told him that if something like this ever happened again, he should not expect to get off so easily.

15

At four thirty that afternoon, Bob Schmidt popped back into the office. "Hope I'm not being too pushy here Dexter. I just have a busy schedule coming up in a few weeks, so you may be waiting a while if I don't start on this stuff now. I could probably do most of the work on weekends too, if you don't want us here during business hours."

"Well Bob, things just slowed down considerably for me, for now. So maybe we better get to it. And, the boys do good work for you?"

"Sure. They're fine. I don't let them do any of the real carpentry. I do all that and have them carrying lumber and sheetrock and cleaning-up and painting. They are pretty good painters.

"And, I really am sorry about how they acted earlier today with that gal in here. I thought I was going to have to turn a hose on them."

"Boys will be boys, especially those two boys. How long do you think it will all take?"

"I think I can get it all done in the next two days, then we come back in on Saturday and paint it all for you. We can get that done in half a day or less."

Dexter told Gina about Bob's plans and let her know she could be as flexible as she wanted with the rest of the week. "You are part time with the county. As long as you get those hours in, I don't care when you are here. And, if they are going to tear the back office up, I will have to sit up here in the front anyway. I might as well answer the phones." With that, they closed the office and headed to The Pawnee Club so Gina could work her shift and Dexter could drink.

"Just go home and watch TV tonight, both of you. I don't know what's wrong with the two of you. But, I don't want either of you in here tonight." Sam Hagan was glaring at Pat and Teddy and pointing toward the door. The pair looked like scolded children and skulked out of the bar. Gina just shook her head and strapped on her apron. She wasn't interested in hearing about that situation but was glad she wouldn't have to deal with those two all night.

Dexter swiveled into a bar stool and watched the two leave. "What was that all about?"

"Those two, my God. Harley Parker was in here, in a mood, but just wanting to drink and be left alone. And those two start in on him about his sister and that kid and something that happened at your office today. I almost had to pull him off the two of them and then he stormed out of here. Then, the other two started in on each other all over again just like last time they got into it, so I sent them out of here."

"Well, that's fine with me, I'm stuck with them the rest of the week while they help Bob Schmidt in my office. And, I feel so bad for Harley right now. I'll have a whiskey barkeep. And a beer back."

Sam poured Dexter his Jack Daniels over some ice and brought a bottle of Busch Light. The bar was empty now, except for a couple of cowboys shooting pool in the back. Sam was in a mood himself and he cut loose. "I don't feel one damn bit sorry for Harley Parker, or his sister. All I ever do is stand back here and pour drinks for people bitching about baby daddies and baby mommas or their kids who are driving them crazy when they have five kids with three different partners and none of them have ever been married.

"Remember when having babies out of wedlock was a big deal? I remember. Then, these girls started getting pregnant and their relatives would say 'She's keeping it,' and people would say 'Well, are they getting married?' And mom or grandma or who whoever would say 'No,' and then someone would say 'Well, at least she isn't having an abortion.'

"I know abortions aren't right, but why does that get to be the excuse to go out and have one kid after another? No one respects marriage anymore and now you got all these kids running around, getting in trouble, cause they only have one parent at home and she is working all the time or running around with her boyfriend of the week."

Gina and Dexter had both heard this rant many times. It was just one of many things that Sam hated about the world. It was compounded by the fact that in his line of work, Sam had to listen to other opinions all night, but was not supposed to offer his own. Sometimes he boiled over and had to vent. Gina winked at Dexter and turned to Sam. "Well, enough of that Sam. Tell us what you think of Dances with Wolves."

Dexter shot Gina a look of incredulous horror. He was in no mood for the rant about how Kevin Costner and the Sioux conspired to vilify the Pawnee on the silver screen.

"God damn it, don't even get me started on that today girl." Sam found himself in apoplectic verbal gridlock and stormed into the cooler to move beer around and cool off.

Gina laughed. "We can't have him going off like that around here. He'll run off all his regular customers."

Dexter shook his head, chugged his beer and put the empty bottle next to his empty whisky glass. "Well, you ran him off, so you need to get me my beer."

****

Relinquishing parental rights takes about two hours of filling out paper work. The process is usually done in a back conference room at Health and Human Services. The case worker may or may not be there with a special HHS worker who only does relinquishments. The parent relinquishing is there, and the parent's attorney. Gracie June

Parker was surrounded by these people as well as her brother.

Dexter had been to his share of relinquishments. They were the saddest things lawyers like Dexter did on a somewhat regular basis. Even if the parent is a really bad parent, he or she is still a parent who loves their child. The only parent the child has ever known. This person now must sit down and coldly and clinically fill out paper work and answer questions that will end a relationship as certainly as death.

Dexter realized how lucky Gracie June was. Sure, she was sad, but her own mental deficiencies made her immune to the full gravity of the situation. She would be sad, but she would get over it, like a child gets over losing a puppy. Harley would not get over it so easily.

The questions were mostly about family medical history and the like. Whether she would ever want the child to contact her. Anything she could tell about the father. Any talents that Gracie June or the family had that might get passed on. Sometimes an adopted child was good at sports or music or art and always wondered if their biological parents had possessed the same talents.

Gracie June could remember that she liked to draw turtles in the sixth grade. So, she wrote that down.

Toward the end, Gracie June got a little bored and anxious to be done. She became agitated and then silly. An hour and a half of this was more than she could handle. She was like a little child who had sat too long in church. It was annoying, but everyone tried to be patient and overlook the behavior. She was giving up her baby.

It was Harley who finally snapped and almost hit his sister. "Just come on Gracie. This is serious."

The case worker spoke up to soothe things. "Grace, I know this is hard and we've been at it a while now, but, I promise, ten more minutes and we are done."

Then, it was done. A lady from the front desk was called in with her notary stamp. Gracie signed, Dexter signed, the workers signed as witnesses and the notary signed and stamped. Everything to make it official. There would be a five-minute hearing in a few weeks and the judge would ask Gracie June if she signed the papers of her own free will with an attorney to advise her. Then, it would all be over.

Dexter walked back to his office, stopping for a twelve-pack. When he got back to the office, Bob Schmidt and the boys had the new walls framed-in and were cleaning up for the day. "Well, Dexter, we should have the drywall up tomorrow by noon. Then we'll put the primer and texture on in the afternoon and it should be ready to paint on Saturday."

"Sounds good Bob. You want a beer?"

"Oh, I'm not supposed to have one very often. Diabetes you know. But, I haven't had one in quite a while. Thanks."

Dexter handed Bob the beer and turned to Pat and Teddy. They were salivating like Pavlov's dogs. He was tempted to not offer them one, just to mess with them. But, he couldn't. The four of them sat in the back office, admiring the work Bob and the boys had done that day and just visited. Dexter enjoyed the company.

"Man," Teddy said, "Sure glad you needed this work Dexter. Pat and me tried to talk to ole Don Birch yesterday to see if he needed any help with anything and Linda practically chased us off her front yard. Said if they needed us, she or Will Jorgensen would call us. She said we needed to leave Don alone."

"Yeah," Pat added, "Poor Don was just sitting on the porch with Will and Linda Jr, looking like his dog just died."

"Looked like that kid they stuck in our class back in eighth grade."

"What kid?"

147

"You remember. That kid who sat in his wheel chair staring at the wall, just kind of moaning. He kept shitting himself."

"Oh, yeah. The teacher had to keep wiping spit of his chin. No, Don ain't that bad. Not yet."

Bob Schmidt looked down into his beer like there might be a dirty picture at the bottom to see. He pressed his lips together like he was going to say something thoughtful, but he didn't. He crushed the empty can and tossed it into his big scrap bucket. He put his hands on his knees and pushed himself up. "Thanks Dexter. Do I need to run these two out of here with me?"

Pat and Teddy looked to Dexter like little kids begging to stay up past bedtime.

"No Bob. They need to help me finish these."

They drained the last beers about an hour later and Dexter wondered if they should head down to The Pawnee Club or just send one of the boys down for more beer. Then Pat spoke-up. "Thanks Dexter." Teddy looked up and nodded in agreement.

"Hell boys, I couldn't drink this beer all by myself."

"Not, just that. For letting us hang out here with you. When we used to work for Jeff and Don, Jeff would once in a while get some beer and we would sit around at the end of the day like this. Bob's a good guy, we just don't visit after work like this, like we used to do with Jeff."

"Jeff AND Don," Teddy corrected. "And, now that Jeff is gone, and we don't work for Don anymore, you and Sam are the only guys around now who treat us like grown men."

Pat now nodded his agreement, "Yeah Dexter. You know, you are nothing at all like any other lawyer I ever knew."

Dexter had heard this said about himself many times before. This was the first time it ever felt like a compliment.

He pulled a twenty out of his pocket and sent the two down the street for more beer.

The boys weren't that smart, but they weren't always annoying either. They had good hearts. They had been relegated to life's back row, and from there they had watched everything. Dexter remembered that it was Teddy who first questioned Don Birch's guilt. He was also the only person to remember that Judge Anderson was an actual human being.

"Hey, Dexter. Me and Teddy were wondering if you could help us with something."

"Sure," As soon as Dexter said "sure" he realized he should have said "it depends" or some other such thing. Oh well, how bad could it be?

"Well, you see, we found this guy down in North Platte who will let us take karate classes from him a couple of days a week. All we have to do is go in a couple of hours early and clean the place and then he will only charge us half price.

"But, we don't have a car to get over there. But, we have found one we can afford."

"Well, Pat. That sounds pretty good. But, I know folks around here have always discouraged you two from getting a car."

"Yeah, well, see. That's where you come in. No one wants us to drive because they think we will do something stupid, like get a DWI."

"Yeah" Teddy said, "or cruise chicks and knock-up every woman in town."

"Yes" agreed Dexter "That always has been a big concern around here."

"Well, anyway. If you would go with us to make sure we aren't getting ripped-off, and then if you would hold the keys and only give them to us when we have to go to karate class or someplace else like that, maybe no one would mind us having a car."

It seemed silly on its face. Pat and Teddy were grown men and could go out and buy a car like any other grown men. But, Pat and Teddy also knew that Sam Hagan would cut them off for good at The Pawnee Club if they bought a car, the local agents would not sell them insurance for the car. And, the deputies would hound them constantly when they were on the road. Dexter mulled all this over. Pat and Teddy were like little kids. Everyone treated them like little kids, but no one ever wanted to take real responsibility for the two. Why should they suffer?

"You know boys, I need to run this by Sam. You know that. But, I'm not just going to tell you no. Let me think on it."

The boys sat back, satisfied. They knew what Sam thought of the idea. Sam had suggested they talk to Dexter, after he had turned them down himself.

16

Dexter came into the office Friday morning to find Gina already there. She had his altered suits hanging on a coat tree in the corner and she was going through files.

"I didn't think you would be in today."

"Yeah, I had your suits ready and I do have two more hours to put in for the county, so I thought I would just come in this morning and run the errands and check your mail. The office looks great."

"Yeah, Bob did a good job. They just have to come in tomorrow and paint and they're done."

Gina went to the post office and courthouse while Dexter read the news online and looked at his calendar for the coming week. He was getting more and more cases appointed to him now and it wasn't helping that he and everyone else were at the mercy of visiting judges. Dexter also saw that he had three bankruptcy hearing coming up. He knew it was easy money, Gina did all the real work and his presence at the hearings was just a formality. Still, they made him nervous. He just needed to have a hearing and once he had one or two under his belt, he would be fine.

Gina came back from the courthouse. Mercifully, there were no new cases. But, she did have a notice of hearing set for Monday on the matter of Don Birch's bond. Dexter looked it over and then looked up Phil Taft's number. Once he got through to Phil, he had a bomb shell dropped on him. "Yeah, Dexter. I didn't take that case. Hell, that poor man came in here with his wife, his daughter and daughter's new beau. They weren't going to let him get a word in edge-wise. And after what you told me the other day and what I got from Wilbur, hell. I turned them down flat."

"Well, I wonder where that leaves me now."

"My guess, it puts you in the driver's seat. Now they know that any lawyer they get will treat this case just like you have been. Just like they don't want."

"Well, thanks. I guess. I don't know what the fuck I'm thanking you for. I really wanted out of this. But, after talking to you, maybe they'll back off with me a little."

"Well, sorry man. You're in it to the very end now. Good luck."

Next, Dexter called Don to tell him about the hearing and what Wilbur would be trying to do. Don was quiet. There was no mention of Phil Taft. Near the beginning of the call, Dexter thought he heard a click, like someone was picking up an extension to listen in. Maybe he was just paranoid. He ignored the click.

Half way into the call, Dexter decided to put pressure on Don again. "Look Don, I need to know what is going on. And you can't keep telling me it's nothing. Your family won't even let you talk to Pat Blocker and Teddy Pickrell. What the hell?"

Don kept playing dumb, but he agreed to meet Dexter for coffee on Monday morning before the hearing. "Look" Dexter explained. "The judge is going to do what he's going to do on this motion to modify the bond. There is really nothing for us to prep for. I just need to make a better argument than Wilbur. But I don't think it matters. The Judge already knows about the hearing and he's probably made his mind up already as to what he is going to do."

The Pawnee Club had a typical crowd for a Friday night, which meant it was pretty packed. Friday was always their busiest night. At about eight thirty, a rare lull hit the place where everyone seemed to have at least half a drink in front of them at once and no one needed Sam for anything. So, he and Dexter were chewing the fat when all hell broke loose. Will Jorgensen was standing over Pat and Teddy at their usual back table. He raised his voice suddenly to Teddy causing everyone else in the place to shut up and turn their way. Just as that silence hit, Will Jorgensen had Teddy by the collar and was slapping him up-side the head as Pat was reaching in to try to stop it.

Now, Dexter had seen Sam come around the bar plenty of times to break-up fights. But, until now, Dexter had never seen Sam come over the bar. Seeing Sam do this out of the corner of his eye stunned Dexter enough that the next thing he realized was that Sam Hagan had Will Jorgenson by the back of his belt and the back of his collar and was pushing Will's face into one of the wooden support posts scattered throughout the bar repeatedly in jab-like motions. The whole bar was stunned silent. After three or four of the jabbing motions that put Will's face into the post, Will was on his back on the floor with Sam's foot in his chest. Will's nose was split open along the bridge and his eyes may have already started to swell shut. It was hard to tell about the swelling though because of all the blood, which was bubbling out of the nostrils as well as coming from the gash on the nose. In the shadows on the floor, all of the blood streaming across Will's face kind of looked to Dexter like Will Jorgensen was wearing a lucha wrestling mask. This made Dexter realize that he was going to want some street tacos when the bar closed, and he wondered if the truck would be out tonight.

No one quite heard what Sam was saying to Will at that point, but Will seemed to be taking it seriously. Whatever it was, it was interrupted when a hulking figure in a plaid shirt and a flat top stepped out of the shadows to loom over both of them. It was Chief Deputy Bob Anderson. It had taken everyone a moment to realize it, but it was definitely Bob Anderson. People were not used to seeing the man out of uniform. And no one would ever expect him to hang out in The Pawnee Club on a Friday night. He had been standing quietly against the back wall, no one knew for how long or why.

"Sam. Take your foot off him and go get him some towels and ice for his nose." It was a forceful command that everyone felt a natural urge to try to obey somehow. It wasn't loud or mean, it was just penetrating and irresistible. Sam complied.

As Bob pulled Will to his feet, Will suddenly found himself emboldened. "Well, deputy. What are you going to do about this?"

"Well, Will, I guess I'm going to leave that up to Teddy." Bob Anderson turned to Teddy. "So, Pickrell, do you want me to cite Jorgensen here for assaulting you, or do you think he's learned his lesson?"

Normally, letting Teddy make a decision like that would be as dangerous as giving a loaded gun to a drunk monkey. But, even Teddy could read in Bob's voice what he was supposed to do. "Well, Bob, I suppose we could let it slide this one time." Teddy smirked at Will and turned back to Bob "As long as Will here understands that next time you and Sam may not be around to break us up. I won't go as easy on him as Sam did."

Will turned and headed for the door stopping at a table near the front to grab Linda, Jr. by the arm and take her out with him. At least now Dexter knew he wasn't paranoid, someone had listened in on his phone call to Don.

Sam was hot. He locked himself in his cooler. Dexter had been around long enough and was good enough friends with Sam that it was natural for him to jump behind the bar and help out in a pinch once in a great while. This was one of those times.

The crowd was a bit too much for Dexter to handle the bar on his own. So, he and Gina ran it together and the patrons came to the bar for their own drinks for about forty-five minutes, until Sam could collect himself and he reappeared. By that time, Dexter wasn't in much mood to drink. So, he just stayed behind the bar and took beer orders while Sam made the mixed drinks and Gina got back out on the floor. Sam never said so, but he seemed to appreciate

154

having Dexter behind the bar with him even though he could have handled things himself.

At last call, Dexter yelled to Teddy and Pat, gave them forty bucks and sent them out to look for the taco truck. About the time the lights came on, as Gina was getting glasses off the table and shooing the last customers toward the door, Pat and Teddy appeared with four little, greasy, brown paper sacks. Bob Anderson came back in three steps behind them.

Everyone gathered at the bar and Sam handed out cans of pop. Dexter passed out the tacos. To be polite, he offered Bob Anderson one, and to everyone's surprise, Bob accepted.

"Bob," Sam said between sips of a Coke "that was quite a lucky coincidence that you decided to come in here, tonight of all nights."

"Not really. I was heading home tonight and saw Will and Linda Jr. out driving around and just decided to follow them a bit."

"Linda was here too?"

"Yup. When I followed them in, she was at the table by the front door and he was over there having words with Teddy."

"What started that Teddy?" Gina wanted to know.

"Honestly, I'm not sure."

"I am." Dexter volunteered. And Dexter proceeded to tell the rest of them about what Pat and Teddy had told him and the following phone call with Don.

Bob nodded his head, absorbing it all and then turned to Teddy. "So, what happened in here tonight when Will approached you?"

"Well, I didn't know what the hell it was all about until I heard what Dexter just told us. I guess it makes sense now."

"What makes sense? What got him so fired-up?"

"Well, I saw him and Linda Jr. come in, and they went to sit at that first table, where you said you saw Linda Jr. sitting. But Will looked up and saw me just as his ass was hitting the chair and he popped back up and made a beeline right at me."

That much talking and recalling was hard work for Teddy just then, especially after drinking all night. He stopped to take a bite of taco.

"Well?" Bob was getting irritated with Teddy, but Teddy didn't seem to notice because he took another bite of taco.

"Swallow that bite and then tell me the rest of the story." Bob commanded, his hand now around Teddy's wrist that held the taco. Startled, Teddy swallowed hard. "Can, I wash it down first?"

Bob let go of Teddy's wrist. Teddy put the taco down, took a long drink of Coke, burped louder than he intended to, said "excuse me" wiped his mouth with the back of his sleeve, and continued his story.

"Well, he just came over all of a sudden like and grabbed me and said, 'You have a big fucking mouth.' So, I said, 'You really ought to see my dick sometime.' And that's when he started slapping me and Sam came over and took matters in hand before I tore Will Jorgensen a new asshole."

"Yeah," Pat said, "Teddy's been working on his over-head hammer strike, and if he had been standing up and Will Jorgensen were six inches shorter. Man, I just hate to think about what Teddy would have done to him."

Bob had heard more than enough from the two. He turned to Dexter. "Mr. Smith, I think your client would be better off in jail. Safer, I mean. It would be for his own good."

"I understand Bob. And you may be right. But I don't get to do what I think is best for him. I do what he tells me to do; to an extent."

****

Monday morning Dexter decided to go ahead and wear one of the newish suits. It fit pretty well. He almost wished he had gotten some new shirts and ties to go with them. But, there would be time for that later.

Dexter met Don Birch for coffee a little before nine that morning in his newly painted office and proceeded to spill the coffee on his lap, staining the pants of the new suit.

"Oh, man. Dexter. You didn't burn yourself, did you?"

"No, I'm alright. Damnit. I just ruined my new suit. Damnit."

"Well, I'm sure you can get it out."

"Yeah, it's the last thing I'm going to worry about right now though. I can go change before court. Now, as for court, you understand what they are trying to do about your bond?"

"Yeah, I think so. But, I haven't tried to run or anything and I've known for a while now that I'm not dying. So, what has changed all of a sudden?"

"Well, nothing really and that is going to be our argument. And it's a good argument to make in a situation like this."

Don had come without his wife or anyone else. Dexter was a little surprised at this but then thought about how awkward it would be for Linda and the rest of the family. They probably assumed Dexter knew of the consultation with Phil Taft. And then there was the dust-up at The Pawnee Club between Teddy and Will Jorgensen. Dexter was quite at ease with just Don and decided to speak freely.

"Don. They are looking to squeeze you. They now believe that things are a lot more complicated in your case than everyone first thought. I have to tell you, I agree with them. I wish you would tell me what's going on, so I can help look after your interests. But I understand that maybe something else is going on, maybe you are looking after someone else's interest. And I just can't do that. You are my client and my only interest in all of this. I am also an officer of the court, and I can't perpetrate a fraud on the court if I know that you are hiding something.

"The sheriff and the county attorney are also looking out for your best interest. Sort of. They think you are in danger. They think you will be safer in jail, and more likely to come clean about what is going on here."

Don smiled at Dexter and tried to laugh off what he had just heard. But he couldn't. He just wasn't that good at deception. His smile went away, and he looked down. He knitted his brows and looked back up at Dexter. "I think we understand each other Dexter. I trusted you from the beginning and I still do. You've done nothing but right by me. And I understand what you can and can't do. So, I understand what I can and can't tell you.

"I also understand that I can't testify, for a lot of reasons. But mostly, the confession. And, we got no other witnesses to help us. So, I'll meet you in court today and you do what you can to keep me out of jail and you keep doing what you need to do to bring all of this to an end. We don't need to meet any more. You just make sure I get all the court dates."

Dexter was ambivalent. He was horrified to think what all Don was hiding from him. And, he was scared for Don. But, he was also relieved to get absolution from Don. There was going to be no resolution in all of this without a total shit storm. A shit storm that would cover the sheriff and his chief deputy, a shit storm that would cover Wilbur Pedersen, just as he was trying to ascend the County Court Bench. It was a shit storm that would cover Don Birch and his family. If Dexter played his cards right, he could maybe get away with only a little shit on his own shoes and nothing more.

Dexter changed out of his grey suit pants and into a pair of black Dickies that somewhat matched the suit coat. He gave the pants to Gina to take to the cleaner's and headed off to court.

The hearing went as everyone expected. Judge Ostergart looked to Don's behavior over the past couple of months he had been on an OR bond and said he saw no reason to change the bond now. Don's safety and speculation of a greater conspiracy were not relevant arguments by law to raise to get the bond increased, so Wilbur didn't bother bringing those up. Wilbur didn't expect to win this hearing, but he had to try it. And, he needed to put pressure on Don's family and Will Jorgensen to help the sheriff and Bob Anderson.

After making his ruling, the Judge, in his usual fashion, asked Wilbur Pedersen if there were anything else. Wilbur responded in the negative. He next turned to Dexter. "Is there anything else Mr. Smith?"

"Yes, Your Honor. In the matter of the second case, the charge of murder of Jeff Hays. We are prepared for trial as soon as possible."

Once again, Wilbur was taken off his feet by Dexter in court. "Your Honor, we were hoping to try the other matter first. We've not sent out jury notifications. And, we haven't had depositions yet. I don't even have Mr. Smith's witness list."

"Mr. Smith?"

"Your Honor. I don't have any witnesses for that case. I don't require depositions right now for that case. And, my client waives his right to a jury trial and would ask that the Court hear the matter. And, as far as order goes, I don't think the state can chose that. I'm just guessing on that. I don't have any case law or procedural rule to back it up."

"I'm guessing you are right about that myself. Unless Mr. Pedersen knows of some law or rules on the matter. Now, Mr. Birch, your attorney has just told me that you want to waive your right to a jury trial and have this case decided by me alone. Is that correct?"

"Yes, Your Honor."

"Has anyone pressured you to waive your right to a jury trial?"

"No, Your Honor."

"Do you understand that a right to a jury trial is an absolute right, guaranteed by the Constitution of the United States and only you can give up that right, no one else can give it up for you or take it away from you?"

"I understand."

"I find that Mr. Birch has knowingly and intelligently waived his right to a jury trial in the presence of his attorney. Mr. Pedersen, how soon can you be ready for trial?"

"I need at least two weeks Your Honor."

"Mr. Smith?"

"I'm ready when the state is."

"Very well, I have two days available starting three weeks from today." Hearing no objections to that date, the Judge set the matter for a trial to the court in three weeks and adjourned the hearing.

Don and Dexter stood to leave and shook hands. It was then that Dexter noticed the two Lindas and Will Jorgensen scurrying out of the back of the courtroom. Before, they had always sat in the front, right behind the defense table. Dexter had not even noticed them until now.

Wilbur Pedersen's office took on the aura of a war room when he shut the door and sat down with Dennis Coffee and Bob Anderson. "Well, what more do you two have on the Hays murder?"

"Not a damn thing Will. And it's not for lack of effort." Said Coffee.

"The problem is, we HAD a confession until I screwed that pooch, so we stopped looking too soon."

"Don't beat yourself up Bob. If this had gone smoothly, Don Birch would be convicted of three murders, dead of cancer and we would have guilty parties walking the streets Scot-free."

"They are going to get away with it anyway."

"What about the GSR on Don?"

"We didn't do one because there was a powder-activated nail gun in his truck he had used that morning."

"Ballistics?"

"Not conclusive. That bullet fragmented in Jeff Hays so bad the ME isn't even sure he got it all out. Besides, we can't even put the gun in Don's hand."

"It was his gun."

"You ever borrow your old man's gun?"

"What about the Roy Musgrave case?"

"That Mexican disappeared like a fart in the wind." Bob said. "I got nothing on him but a fake name and social. I'm not even sure he's Mexican. He's only five one and he wears a mullet. So, I'm guessing he's a Guat."

Wilbur and Sheriff Coffee absorbed what Bob Anderson had just said. The Sheriff turned to Wilbur "What do you want us to do now?"

"Well, at this point we're pretty sure there's more than one rat here. Hell, Don's probably the least culpable. Maybe it's time we turn his case into a sacrifice fly and squeeze the others a little. We're going to lose this one, probably both cases. Let's add the daughters to the witness list, subpoena them to testify against dad and see what happens."

"Even if we lose, we could re-charge Don for aiding and abetting if we can prove a conspiracy. No jeopardy there, right Will?" Wilbur looked at Sheriff Coffee and nodded an affirmative.

Bob Anderson was livid. "I'm just sorry as hell you're going to lose a case to that damn Dexter Smith because of me. How the hell did he even get to be a lawyer? Is there a short bus that goes to law school?"

17

The next two weeks went by unremarkably for Dexter. Gina was running the office and him. He just showed-up at the office, signed what she told him to sign, went to court when she sent him and met with clients and potential clients she scheduled appointments with.

He could not tell if the criminal cases had taken a dip or if they were just smother with Gina around. He had gotten the hang of bankruptcy cases and was doing a couple of those a week. He had also taken on a couple of divorce cases.

He went with Pat and Teddy one day to look over their "new" car. Technically it was a car. It was a 1980 Ford Pinto station wagon. The guy selling it went into great detail about all the work he had done when he had restored it to its original show-room condition, just ten years ago. Pat and Teddy were in love. Dexter remembered being this excited about his first car, but he had been fifteen at the time.

Dexter had not seen or heard from Don Birch since their last hearing. Dexter had done little to prepare for the trial. All he would have to do was poke holes in a very circumstantial case and create reasonable doubt. Then came Wilbur's motion to endorse more witnesses in the case. Namely, Linda Hays and Delores Stubbs.

"Gina, do you know a Delores Stubbs?"

"Yeah, Dorrie Stubbs, she works at the bowling alley."

Dexter called Wilbur Pedersen. Wilbur agreed to fax over the statement that Dorrie Stubbs had provided to Bob Anderson. Wilbur didn't have a statement from Linda Hays, which didn't surprise Dexter. It was a fishing expedition, Wilbur was going to put Linda Jr. on the stand, have her sworn in and just see what happened. Dexter could guess that whatever Linda Jr. was asked would have a lot to do with what Dorrie had to say. Wilbur would probably call Linda

Jr. after Dorrie took the stand. It was a smart move on Wilbur's part and it didn't bother Dexter any because Dexter had a good idea that he was doing all of this to go after Linda Jr. and possibly her mother and Will Jorgensen.

Dexter did worry about what the Lindas and Will Jorgensen would do to Don when they got wind of all of this. Dexter also wondered about Don's other daughters. He couldn't remember ever seeing either of them in court. But, he also wasn't sure what they looked like, so they could have been in court at some time and him not even know it.

Dexter decided to go see Tom McWilliams. As far as Dexter knew, Tom was still ass deep in the Musgrave estate and would probably know more about Marcia Musgrave than anyone else. Whatever Marcia's position in the estate, she wasn't Tom's client, so Tom should be pretty free to share what he knew about her.

Dexter found Tom in his conference room going over several stacks of files spread out on the table. They were all Musgrave files. Tom looked up at Dexter and smiled. Tom was looking for an excuse to take a break. "Hey Dex, let's go get a coffee."

The two settled into a back table at the diner and ordered coffee and pie. "I saw the bankruptcy docket for next month Dex. You have quite a few cases going. How many years have you been telling me that you would never do bankruptcies because you would never understand them?"

"Well, that was before Gina. I still don't know the first damn thing about them. I guess I can learn. I can't let her do all the work. "

"They aren't that hard, mostly bookkeeping and administrative, dotting your 'I's and crossing your 'T's. Gina knows all that stuff. You can pick up what you need to. Just don't start taking on farm or corporate bankruptcies, at least not until you think you are ready. Don't let Gina get you in over your head. Truth be told, I don't understand them as much as my clients probably think I do. "

"Well, I hope I'm not taking any of that business away from you."

"Hell no, I'm sending you most of the ones I'm getting now. I want to be ready to move into Will's office as soon as it opens-up for me. I gotta get this Musgrave estate settled and closed as soon as you finish up your end. I don't want any more loose ends than necessary when it comes time for the move."

"Well, you and Wilbur sure seem sure of yourselves. Are you sure you two aren't putting the cart way before the horse here? Maybe the court administrators will say we don't need a judge. The visiting judges seem to be doing alright."

"The court administrators have already approved the vacancy, they did that last week. And, Wilbur is the only one who has put in for it. Except for a few who always put in for judgeships and never get them. And, I don't want this to go any further, but two of the commissioners have already told me and Wilbur that I have their support to fill Wilbur's office until the next election. They did that when they approved your contract. You are always the pessimist Dexter. You need to think more positively. You need to trust me and Wilbur.

"You know, Dexter, my plans are to move up to the District Court bench as soon as Ostergart retires. You need to start thinking about moving into the County Attorney position yourself when that happens."

Dexter choked on his coffee and a little came out of his nose. Tom's suggestion sounded nothing short of absurd. He tried to regain his composure to tell Tom so, but Tom had already gotten the point.

"Look, Dexter. Three months ago, would have guessed that you would be handling a murder case, and handling it well, while you were building a bankruptcy practice?"

"No, but"

165

"But, nothing. Dexter, you have always been your own worst enemy. All that 'hick lawyer' crap. You don't know everything there is to know about the law. Do I? Does Will Pedersen? Does Judge Ostergart or anyone else for that matter? Hell no. Look at Judge Anderson. Worst legal mind in Nebraska history. Did that stop him from having a pretty successful career on the bench? Hell no. We all figure it out and do it. We develop habits, just like you are doing with bankruptcies now. You will be surprised at what you know about bankruptcies in a couple of months. You are on the other side of most of Wilbur's cases right now, you can handle his side too. And, anything you can't do or don't want to do, just give it to one of those deputy county attorneys. They love to do the research and all of that administrative law bullshit."

Dexter had to absorb all of this. He was now doing more with his practice than he ever thought he would. "Well, I'll think about it. I guess I have plenty of time to do that. But, in the meantime, I have to see this Birch case through. What do you know about Marcia Musgrave and her sisters and mother?"

"I'm paying Marcia's bills until the estate settles and the trusts are dissolved and dispersed. She's living in Lincoln in an efficiency for now. She is close to the kids and her doctors. I know what you are thinking about her mother and sisters. Everyone is talking about them. Whatever is going on, I don't think Marcia has anything to do with it. Whatever it is. And I don't think Debra Miller does either. Rumor has it she's drinking herself to death. She quit teaching and is living off Scott's life insurance, which won't last her too long. She is one hot mess.

"Marcia had to come back to town a couple of weeks ago to go over some stuff with me. About a half hour after we finished up, I came down here for lunch, and she and Don and Debra were having lunch together. Just the three of them. Whatever they were talking about was pretty heated.

But they clammed-up as soon as they saw me walk in. Before I was finished with my lunch, Marcia kissed them both and was headed out the door."

"Where do things stand with the estate right now?"

"As soon as the trustees are satisfied that Marcia had nothing to do with Roy's death, which I think will be soon, I dissolve everything, pay the taxes and set her and the kids up. Most of what I am doing now is busy work, getting the taxes in order and all so everything is ready to file and close as soon as the trustees give me the nod."

"Well, if Marcia and Debra had nothing to do with any of this, why haven't they come to me or the sheriff to help their dad out?"

"They are probably as scared of their mother and their little sister as everyone else. And, I would guess that Don won't let them. When Don married Linda 'for better or worse,' he took that vow very seriously."

Dexter got back to the office and found Dorrie Stubbs' written statement in the fax machine, along with Bob Anderson's supplemental report on Dorrie Stubbs. Dexter did not know quite what to make of it. The gist of it was that Dorrie had seen Linda Jr. and Will Jorgensen having drinks in the bowling alley lounge on a regular basis for the last six months on the nights that Linda Jr. and her mother had regularly bowled together. Linda Sr. sometimes joined them. Three nights before the murders, both Lindas and Will Jorgensen were engaged in a very intense conversation in a back booth of the lounge. On the night of the murders, Linda Sr. was there all night, while Linda Jr. and Will Jorgensen were in and out of the place, sometimes together, sometimes at different times.

Dexter didn't know exactly what all of this meant, but he knew where it was headed. Wilber was not going after Don at all. But, how was Wilbur going to get this in? None of this would be relevant to the case against Don.

167

Dexter would have to object to all the testimony Wilbur tried to elicit about this as irrelevant. None of this would get in at trial. Maybe Wilbur knew this too. Maybe Wilbur was trying to make something happen before the trial. Dexter would have to share this information with Don. But first, he wanted to talk to someone. He called Tom McWilliams and asked him for Marcia Musgrave's phone number.

"Mr. Smith, I am surprised to hear from you. I thought you were instructed not to talk to me."

"Well, Mrs. Musgrave, I was only instructed to talk to your father and your mother about your father's case. I have not been given permission to discuss the case with anyone else."

"But, has that changed? Has Dad finally told you to talk to me about his case?"

"No, he has not. He doesn't know I am calling you. I am not able to tell you anything about the case. But, I thought that maybe there was something that you wanted to tell me about the case. You see, I can't answer questions about your father's case, but I can ask questions. That is what I am doing now. So, is there anything you can tell me that will help your father?"

"Like what?"

"I don't know. I thought that maybe you would know what you need to tell me."

"I'm not sure what would help. What I can say is that I know that my father never killed anyone. He couldn't. My father certainly could never have killed Jeff Hays. Not even my mother could make him do that. And you have no idea what kind of things my mother could make my father do. What she is capable of making any of us do."

"Mrs. Musgrave, it sounds like you have a theory about what may have happened. Why don't you just tell me that? I think it would be a big help."

"I think that when Dad got that diagnosis, my mother and my sister saw a way of taking care of all of their problems. And, for good measure, they decided to take care of my problems and Deb's problems, just so they wouldn't have to worry about us.

"Deb and I haven't exactly been told to stay away. But we have been made to feel unwelcome and we know to stay away. That is why I will be buying a house here when Roy's estate settles, and I will be moving Deb here to live with me. If you get our dad out of this, he can come here too. But he won't. He is the only thing Deb and I have left there."

"You make it all seem so diabolical. What are your mother and sister capable of?"

"The Lindas? Mr. Smith, when I was in high school, I had a boyfriend, Tommy Hernandez. Everyone loved Tommy. He was a great kid. Even my mother liked Tommy, but she didn't like me dating a Hispanic boy. She thought that too many people would disapprove, privately of course, but disapprove none the less. She did everything to break us up. Finally, Linda Jr., who was still in elementary school at the time, told my father and her principal that Tommy had touched her one day while he was pushing her on the swing in our back yard. He denied it, I didn't believe it. No one really believed it, but mother. Mother taught at the elementary school, so she and the principal were close. Everyone agreed that if Tommy and his parents could take care of the matter, the police would not be notified. So, Tommy and his family moved to Grand Island. They had relatives there. And, of course, that ended our relationship. After that, whenever Tommy's name came up, the Lindas would give each other a glance. A glance like they had a special secret that only they knew. It was like a game to them. They were so proud of themselves."

"Do you really think they framed Tommy?"

"Mr. Smith. My mother and my sister are capable of anything. They know what they want, and they always get it. And they always want the same thing."

"What about Jeff Hays?"

"When Will Jorgensen left town, after his father died, Linda Jr. was devastated. So was mother. Jeff wasn't from the best of homes. He was a lot like Dad. He was too much like Dad. But he was sure good looking, and he worked hard. They knew he was going to do something with himself. Just like Dad had done. At first, most of us just thought Jeff was a diversion to take Linda's mind off Will. It was surprising when they got married after they finished college. But, he was going to be a businessman. The only problem was, he went into my dad's business, and suddenly that wasn't good enough. My sister always resented being married to someone so much like Dad. Debra and I would have given anything to be married to someone like our dad."

"You think your mother and your sister killed your husbands?"

"With help from Will Jorgensen."

"Why would he go along with it?"

"They are very persuasive women. And Will had his own reasons. He was always a snake in the grass, like the rest of his family. They left town under a cloud. His parents did a lot of shady stuff in their real estate office and were about to lose everything, right before his father died. That is why they left. Between what Roy's trust owns and the houses Jeff owned around town, there is going to be a lot of real estate to sell and property to develop. Will is going to rehabilitate his family's name and take back their real estate business; and make a lot of money at it."

"If I talk to your sister, Debra, is she going to tell me the same thing?"

"Please don't talk to Debra. She can't handle any of this. And, please, do not tell my mother that I spoke to you.

And, if you tell my father that you spoke to me, ask him not to tell her either. I know he won't; but ask him anyway."

Dexter waited a few minutes after hanging up the phone before he called Don. He told Don that there were new developments in the case that he could only talk to Don about. Someone was listening in again. Don asked to call Dexter right back. Twenty minutes later Don called and asked how soon he could get in to see Dexter, he wanted to get in right away. He would come alone.

18

Gina showed Don into Dexter's office late that afternoon. Don walked in with a sense of determination. Right away he wanted to see everything Dexter had in the files. "I want to see it all Dexter, the pictures, the statements. Everything." Dexter started with the pictures of the crime scenes and the evidence collected. Don saw Scott Miller's legs sticking out from under the car. He saw Roy Musgrave's desk covered in Roy's brains. He saw the big mallet with Roy's blood and bits of hair. He saw Jeff siting in his easy chair, Don looked at that picture for a long time. Next, he saw his old .22 single action. Don took this picture between thumb and first two fingers. He held it up close, like he was smelling it. He stared for what seemed like a very long time at that picture too.

"I bought this gun fifty-six years ago. Bought it brand new." Don sat back in his chair and kept looking at the picture of the gun. "I was stationed in Gulfport, Mississippi. I was a Seabee. That's where I learned construction. I got this gun to take fishing. There was some good fishing around there. Not just salt water, but all those creeks and bayous. Lots of cottonmouths though. So, I got this gun for the snakes.

"I got this gun to shoot snakes. I don't think I ever did shoot one though. Hell, it's a fancy looking gun, and it was fun to shoot it at cans. That was the real reason I got it. I was just seventeen or eighteen. I didn't ever wonder what would happen if a snake got ahold of it."

Don chucked the picture back on Dexter's desk and sat back. "Do you have any coffee Dexter?" Dexter got up and poured them each a cup. It had sat all day. But it was hot. They sipped in silence for a minute or two. "Dexter. How far does attorney/client privilege go? I mean, how long does it last?"

"Well, Don. It lasts until you say it doesn't last, or until you die, in certain circumstances. There are other things that end the privilege, but they are all things triggered by you."

"That's what I thought. So, I'm going to just go ahead and tell you everything. And, you're just going to have to sit on it for a while. If the time comes for you to do something about it, you'll know it. And, you'll know what to do."

"But, you know I won't be able to suborn perjury. If you tell me something now, I won't be able to elicit testimony that I know to be false at the trial on Jeff's killing."

"You aren't going to call any witnesses for that, are you? They can't prove that I killed Jeff on the evidence that they have, can they?"

"I don't think they can."

"Do you think I killed Jeff Hays? Does anyone think that? Does anyone really think I was capable of killing Jeff Hays?"

"No. But, you had just gotten some pretty devastating news that day. No one knows what was going through your mind or why you decided to do anything they think you did. And, you confessed Don."

"It was three days."

Dexter stopped. What had Don just said? It took a moment to register what Don had just said and what it meant. Nothing in the reports had indicated when exactly Don had gotten the cancer diagnosis. He had assumed it was the same day as the murders. He had never discussed it with Don. He now understood the importance of Dorie's statement and the three days leading up to the murders that Will Jorgensen and the Lindas had been conspiring about something at the bowling alley.

173

"It was three days after I got the news Dexter. I think a lot of people are confused about that. It was three, crazy, hand-wringing days. My wife and I were reviewing my life insurance policy. Going over all the property deeds. Going over all our finances, my VA benefits. She sure seemed relieved when she saw how well I was gonna leave her.

"You know, Dexter, a lot of people wonder why she married me. The truth is, I don't know. I think the way I came into town and started buying property; maybe she thought I had more money than I did. She thought I came from a better family than I did. I was pretty good looking back then too. Plus, I'd made petty officer before I left the Navy. I think she thought that meant I was an officer." Don sat staring off like he was staring all the way back in time some fifty years.

"Anyway. As soon as we figured out how set up she was going to be, she didn't seem to mind that I was dying. We talked about everything that Jeff could help her do with the houses. I think that's what started getting her nervous and she and Linda Jr. started talking a lot in the back room, lots of whispering by golly. Then, Linda started in on Scott Miller, she knew that would get to me. After what he did to Debra before. She knew that would get under my skin. And when she had me all worked up over that, she started in on Roy Musgrave and how he was liable to up and divorce Marcia at any time and leave her high and dry. It all got me to thinking.

"But, I kept telling them that Jeff would take care of everything and not to worry. I knew that Linda Jr. and Will Jorgensen were sneaking around. I hoped that me dying and Jeff taking over everything would put a stop to that. Then, Linda Jr. showed up at the house with Will and she wanted him to go over all the property deeds. 'Will can help liquidate some of the property for Mom, and Jeff may need help managing your property and his own' she said. I didn't like it. I just walked out of the room and let them go through

174

it all themselves. I didn't even pretend to like it. Then, my lovely wife starts talking about some uncle she had who got a cancer diagnosis, so he went and blew his own brains out to save time and his family's suffering. But, then she told me not to even think about doing that. I knew what she was doing.

"So, three days go by and Linda's still working on me about Scott and Roy, and her uncle keeps coming up. I had some idea of what she was up to, I just couldn't believe it.

"Finally, she says she has to get out and take her mind off things, she decides to go bowling. She tells me I should go see Scott. She has me so worked up, I just go to see him. I pull up in the alley behind his house to go into the garage, and Will Jorgensen pulls right in behind me. I didn't know what the hell to think. He walks up, sticks his and out and says, 'Ms. Linda thought you might need this.' And he's holding that .22. I didn't know what to think. I was just so pissed at all of them at that point. I didn't know any more what I was doing there or what I was going to do. I was crazy Dexter. The reality of everything was just pushing down on me. I walked into the shop. I saw Scott's feet sticking out from under the car. I saw the floor jack. I turned and looked at Will. He just looked at me like he expected me to do something. I just stood there. He tried to hand me the gun again and I just stood there. So, Will walked over, grabbed the floor jack, turned the handle as fast as he could, and we watched the car slam down on Scott. He screamed when the car first started to fall, but he went silent real fast. The next thing I remember, I was walking back into my house and Linda Jr. was there. I went to my room. Will came in behind me and they talked about what had happened. Then I heard Linda Jr. leave and Will came into the bedroom.

"Will told me that it had to be done and it was what my wife wanted. Then, he left, I heard him drive off in my truck, and in a little while, Linda Jr. came back in and tried to hand me the pistol. Will came in behind her and they told me what had happened. Will had killed Roy and she had killed Jeff. She killed her husband with my gun. I sat on the edge of my bed. She laid the gun down next to me and they both walked out.

"I guess I was supposed to shoot myself then. I don't know. I didn't know what to do, but I wasn't going to give them that satisfaction. But, when Bob Anderson showed-up at the house, I just went along with him and told him I did it. I did it all.

"My wife couldn't come out and say it, but she wasn't happy that I hadn't shot myself. Then, we found out I'm not dying. I tell you Dexter, it has been a long, strange few months."

Dexter and Don sat in silence for a while. Dexter did not know what to think. He (and everyone else in town) had known that the Lindas and Will Jorgensen had been involved somehow. It all made perfect sense. Still, Dexter just couldn't absorb it all. What the hell was he going to do now?

Finally, he looked up at Don. "I don't know what the hell to do about all of this. Don, what do you want me to do about all this?"

"Just get me through that trail on Jeff's murder. I want a court of law to say that I'm not guilty of that. That is all I want. My wife and my daughter are getting nervous. They thought, that one way or another, I would die and take all of this to the grave. Then they started to think that you would take care of all of this and it would just somehow go away. But, I think that mostly, now, they think that if I die, it still all goes away. I'm not going to spill the beans on them, but I don't think they trust me not to."

Dexter almost wanted to laugh "spill the beans." Most of Dexter's clients would have said "dime them out." But, that would have sounded even funnier coming from Don. And, there were serious things to consider that Don had just said. "Why would they think that you would die now?

176

You aren't sick. Do you think they would kill you?" Dexter knew the answer to this. They had already killed three men.

"I hope they won't. But, would it matter? I'm either looking at life in prison or spending the rest of my life in this town, ostracized. Besides, once I get cleared of Jeff's death, there is still Roy's. And, there is someone other than my wife and daughter worried about that one. I wouldn't turn my back on Will Jorgensen right now. In fact, I am doing all that I can to avoid the lot of them."

Don got up to leave and Dexter got up to see him out. "Dexter, whatever you think of my family, they are my family. I'm not ready to turn them in."

As they reached the door of the front office, a car pulled up, and, out popped Teddy and Pat. "Dexter. We got it. We got the car. It's a 1980, but it was completely restored to its original showroom condition in 2001."

All the weight on Don seemed to lift as he looked at the 1980 Pinto wagon. He started in on the boys like he always had when they worked for him. "Why in the holy hell would anyone waste time, money, and talent restoring a goddamn Pinto station wagon to its original, showroom condition? Why?"

Pat and Teddy stood beaming. "Isn't it cool?" exclaimed Pat.

"Yeah," said Teddy. "And we're gonna line the back with shag carpet for when we pickup chicks in this thing. It is going to be a real shaggin-wagon."

Don was incredulous. Like Sam Hagan and some of the other men in town, Don had tried to look out for the boys. He felt bad that with everything going on in his life, he had neglected them lately.

The middle aged mutant ninja turtles were not dissuaded. If they had heard what Don had just said, it did not register with them. They beamed with pride at the shaggin-wagon. Don realized that his protests were doing no good, and he also realized that the boys having a car that would break down soon may be a good thing. He let it go and congratulated them on their new car.

"Boys, I'm working on that duplex on the south side, I could use a little help, if you're feeling up to it."

Pat and Teddy beamed, then looked at each other and both became oddly reserved. Teddy spoke up. "Well, Don, we really can't right now, but if you need us tomorrow or the next day, we could make it over to help you for a while."

"Great, I need to hang some ceiling drywall in a couple of rooms. That should only take an hour or so, then you boys can clean-up for me. Just get there by ten tomorrow." Don turned and thanked Dexter again for his time and clapped Teddy and Pat each on the shoulder before climbing into his truck and driving off. They watched him head down the main drag of town, headed south. Dexter turned to admire the boys' new ride. He let them go over every inch of it with him, listening to them regurgitate everything the guy who sold it to them had told them about it.

"Well," Dexter finally said. "You boys must have something pretty important going on to turn Don down on work like that. You taking the shaggin-wagon out to put her through her paces?"

The boys stopped and gave each other the same funny look they had given each other when Don had first asked them for help. "Well," Pat said. "We sure have missed working for Don. But, Will and the Lindas don't want us around him. So, we will just wait until tomorrow, when Will might not be around."

"What do you mean? Don didn't say anything about Will being around. I think Don is trying to avoid Will."

"Well," Said Teddy. "We just drove by the duplex, and Will was pulling in behind the place. Back in the alley, behind it. But we saw him alright. Pat's right. We need to stay away if he's over there today."

Dexter was frozen when he heard this. Given everything Don had just told Dexter, especially what Don had said about Will Jorgensen, this was not good. This was not good at all.

"Boys, I think we need to get down to the duplex. I don't think Don knows Will is down there." Teddy and Pat had never been too quick on the up-take. But, they had heard the rumors around town just like everyone else. They were among the first to proclaim Don's innocence. They did not need Dexter to explain more, which was good, because Dexter really couldn't ethically go into much detail. "We just need to head down there and make sure everything is alright and play it cool if it is. I just need to make a phone call."

Dexter headed into the office and used Gina's phone to call Bob Anderson. He really didn't have to explain much to Bob either. Bob had already predicted that Don should be in fear for his life. This was good, because Bob was out on patrol, but the dispatcher promised to get the message to Bob on his cell phone.

Dexter headed out the door to see that the boys had decided they couldn't wait on him any longer. He looked down the street to see the shaggin-wagon three blocks down, rounding the corner on two wheels. So much for just showing up and playing it cool. Dexter ran back into the office to look for his car keys, which he was pretty sure were on his desk. He was trying to remember the last time he had actually taken his car somewhere and where it was parked.

Pulling out of the parking stall, Dexter realized there was no way he would get there before the boys. He just hoped that Bob Anderson was not on the other side of the county and that the dispatcher had contacted him right away like she had promised. Maybe he should have called 911. No, that would be hard to explain if there was no actual emergency. Of course, if he got there too much after the boys, an emergency situation could develop.

179

Dexter knew exactly what duplex he was going to. It was the duplex he had lived in for three years. It was the only duplex Don owned on the south side of town. He also knew that there had been a kitchen fire in it a few months before and Don was spending a lot of time remodeling it. He and Jeff had put a new roof on it the morning of the day Jeff was killed.

He pulled-up to the curb behind the shaggin-wagon. Don's truck was in the driveway. Dexter caught a glimpse of a car in the alley that was probably Will's. He only saw it because he was looking for it. It was at the back of the back yard behind the shed, pointed toward the alley for a quick getaway. Or, maybe Dexter was just being paranoid.

Dexter wasn't just being paranoid. Half way up the walk to the front door, he heard screams and inaudible yelling over the loud drone of an air compressor. He could also hear periodic thuds, like muffled gunshots. He picked up his pace and put his shoulder to the front door. It wasn't locked, and he stumbled to his knees in the middle of his old living room as the door easily gave way to his excessive force.

When Dexter was sure his momentum had stopped, he looked up from his knees to see Pat Blocker right in front of him, with nails sticking out of his upper arm and his jaw, he was clasping his thigh which had another nail protruding from it. Pat was hovering over Don Birch's body. A nail was deeply imbedded in Don's bloody temple.

Behind Pat and Don, Teddy and Will Jorgensen were wrestling in the kitchen over a pneumatic nail gun. Dexter raced in, lowering his shoulder to plow into Will, but Will spun quickly causing Dexter to instead knock Teddy to the floor, with Dexter going down on top of him, pushing on a nail that was protruding from Teddy's shoulder, causing Teddy to scream. Teddy's scream was soon muffled by Dexter's own scream as two nails shot into his back in quick succession. Nail guns were not supposed to go off unless they were placed directly against something to be nailed. Don and the boys had modified the gun, so they could shoot nails at cardboard targets. Don's powder-actuated gun had been confiscated by Bob Anderson as part of the murder investigation.

Dexter rolled off Teddy to see Will Jorgensen coming toward him with the gun. Pat appeared, swinging a two by four at Will's head, but swung too soon, allowing Will to take a step back and shoot a nail into Pat's belly. Dexter froze, as Will turned back to him ready to shoot another nail, when the compressor went quiet. Everyone turned to see Teddy slumped over the compressor, with the engine choke in his hand. With all the adrenalin, he had managed to pull it completely from the compressor's motor. Dexter saw for the first time that Teddy had managed to shoot a few nails into Will during the scuffle that Dexter had interrupted. The cut on Will's nose from the fight at The Pawnee Club was bleeding again too.

It was now three against one as Dexter and the middle-aged mutant ninja turtles turned to circle Will who had backed into a corner. "Pat," said Dexter. "Go call someone."

"Don't any of you go anywhere," said Will, pulling a small .25 automatic from his pants' pocket. "I didn't want to use this. But I guess it doesn't matter now." He pointed the gun at Pat and motioned him to move over closer to the other two. "I warned you two to stay away from Don. You interrupted his suicide. He didn't want to go on after what he did to Jeff and the others."

"Don didn't kill anyone you lying, sack of shit." Said Teddy "And we saw you driving that nail into his head. You'll pay for this, all of it you bag of shit."

"Shut the fuck up. All three of you, move to the kitchen door. I don't want to drag your bodies any further than I have to. Look at this mess I'll have to clean up before I call in Don's suicide."

181

"What are you going to do with us? Bob Anderson is on his way hear right now." Dexter hoped that Bob was on his way. Even if he didn't get there to save them, once they disappeared, Bob would know what happened and where to start looking. Dexter realized that was not as comforting a thought as he had expected it to be.

"Two retarded kung-foo wanna-bes and the worst lawyer in the world are not going to fuck all this up. Now, move to the door." Dexter watched as Will Jorgensen pointed the gun squarely at the center of Dexter's forehead. It was a small caliber gun, but when pointed directly at him, that barrel looked big.

Teddy was having none of this. He and Pat had been called all kinds of things in their lives, it wasn't nice, but they had gotten used to it. They had been called worse things than Will had just called them, and by worse people than Will. No, wait, Teddy couldn't really think of anyone worse than Will at the moment. But, Dexter Smith was far from the worst lawyer in the world. And, even if he weren't the best lawyer in the world, he was Pat and Teddy's lawyer. He was also their friend. He was one person they could always rely on to treat them like adult, human, men; not retards or little kids. Will Jorgensen was not going to talk to Dexter Smith like that right before killing him.

No one in that room that day was ever able to adequately describe or imitate what came next. Though, they would never forget it. It was a guttural moan; a harrowing, visceral cry, not from the diaphragm or even way down in the guts. It was a sound that emanated from somewhere deeper. It was coming from Teddy Pickrell. Will Jorgensen froze. Pat and Dexter found themselves covered in chills, half expecting something to come up through the floor from the pits of Hell. Teddy grabbed the nail wound in his chest, pumping blood now between his fingers and he marched across the floor, directly at Will Jorgensen. The sound grew louder as he raised his free hand in a fist above his head. The first was a diversion as he planted his left foot firmly in front of himself and spun around backwards, raising his right leg to the height of his head. As his leg came around, his foot just inches from Will's head, Will's gun went off. The bullet caught Teddy in his right side, slowing his momentum, but not enough to prevent contact which caused Will to stagger backward for a second before he regained his balance. Teddy crumpled to the floor. And then the second gunshot went off. The second gunshot was louder than the first. It came from the front door. From the service .38 revolver Bob Anderson had never traded in for a 9mm. It was a true shot in the center of Will Jorgensen's chest. Will grabbed his chest, looked around to gain a split second of clarity of what had just happened to him before he dropped to the floor, stone dead.

19

Dexter and Pat gave their full statements to Sheriff Coffee as soon as the doctor cleared them to do so. One of the nails in Dexter's back had lodged in a rib in his back, just a quarter of an inch from his spine. He was lucky not to be paralyzed. The main concern now was tetanus, which was treated with a shot. He had also badly sprained his knee during one of the multiple spills he had taken in the fracas. He hurt all over. Pat had more nail injuries. Besides the one pulled out of his jaw that was now causing his whole face to swell, they took three out of his torso and one out of his left leg. None had hit any arteries or vital organs, but his third favorite Bruce Lee t-shirt could not be saved. The doctor wanted to keep him in the hospital for observation given the number of nails shot into him. He was going to be too sore to move for a few days. They were both looking at spending at least that night in the hospital.

The nail that hit Teddy in the chest had missed his heart but punctured the lung. His last stand against Will Jorgensen had saved Dexter Smith but had also caused the nail to tear the puncture wound in his lung. The bullet that hit Teddy's side, had gone right through him and lodged in a wall, but had nicked the edge of his liver in the process. The surgeon opted for the exploratory surgery on his guts first, making sure nothing was damaged other than the liver. Then, he went in and patched the lung. Teddy had lost a lot of blood. He was going to be in the hospital for a while. He was expected to make a full recovery, but it was too soon to say if he could ever drink PBR again.

When Teddy was finally able to give his statement, it matched the statement Pat had given. Dexter's statement matched the other two's statements from the point where he arrived on the scene. Pat and Teddy had gotten to the duplex two or three minutes ahead of Dexter. On their way to the front door they had heard the compressor start up and Don yell "What the hell are you doing?" They had pushed their way into the front door pretty much the way Dexter had, the door shutting back on itself from their force. There they saw Will standing behind Don, applying a chokehold to the old man and holding the nail gun to his temple. Pat and Teddy both rushed the other two, but as they got ahold of Don, and Will's arm to pry them apart, the gun went off. Don stiffened, and when Will released the chokehold, Don fell to the floor. While Pat and Teddy were still in shock from the sight, Will began firing, first dropping Pat with the nail to the leg. From there no one could remember the actual sequence too well. But, it didn't matter. Everyone got the picture.

Bob Anderson had gotten the message right away. The dispatcher had not conveyed Dexter's sense of urgency while delivering it, but she didn't need to. Bob knew that if Dexter were contacting him at all, it was serious. Bob had only been halfway across the county when he got the message. He had driven twenty-eight miles in just under fifteen minutes. By all accounts, once on the scene, he had made a righteous kill, one that had saved three lives. His administrative leave was a formality and would not last a month.

Sam Hagan was in and out of Dexter and Pat's room all the following day. Gina came in with her grandmother and Mildred Pedersen. The older two showered them with cookies and afghans crocheted by the women of their church. They doted on Pat, talking about his mother and how proud his father and grandfather would be of him and Teddy, and how they had to promise to never do such a thing again, and they really needed to give up their martial arts nonsense because everyone had warned them over the years that they were just going to hurt themselves, and here, it had happened.

Dexter was glad to be out of there when the doctor finally released him at five that evening. He got Gina to drive him home, where he feasted at Lee Ho Fooks before slowly making his painful way up the stairs and onto his couch.

The next afternoon, Dexter found that Teddy had been moved out of ICU and into the bed Dexter had occupied next to Pat's. They were being visited by a little guy Dexter was sure he had never seen before in his life. It was hard to say what was most striking about the little guy's appearance. He was five-foot, four inches and rail thin, with toothpick arms sticking out of a white, sleeveless Enter the Dragon t-shirt. His hands disappeared into his pockets just below the four-inch leather bands buckled around his wrists. His dirty blonde hair was permed and feathered on top, while the back hung down to between his shoulder blades. The sides of his head were cropped close and had lines and lightning bolts shaved into them. Simply saying this guy had a mullet would be like saying a '68 Corvette was a car. Below his wire-rimmed glasses and hook nose grew a Fu Manchu moustache that reached three inches below his weak chin. This strange, little man was so imposing in his own funny way that Dexter stood in the door staring at him for almost a full minute before he noticed Bob Anderson standing in a corner with his arms crossed, looking like he was going to explode any second.

Pat and Teddy saw Dexter and waived him into the room. "Dexter, this is our new sensei, Bo Brubaker." Dexter turned to the little man and extended his hand, as the little guy snapped to attention, put his hands at his side and bowed deeply to Dexter before extending his own hand to grab Dexter's in a soul shake.

"Dexter Smith. I have just heard all about your ordeal. I sure bet you are glad you had these two with you."

"Yeah, I sure am. If it weren't for Teddy here, Will Jorgensen would have blown my brains out."

"Yeah. I guess so. I thought it was interesting for Teddy to go for that spinning-swing kick in a time like that. But, it just shows that while he has the heart of a true warrior, he lacks formal training in the arts.

"I was just telling these guys that going in low with a leg sweep would have been a safer way to go." Sensei Brubaker turned to Bob Anderson. "Wouldn't you have gone with the leg sweep deputy?"

"No, I would have still used my .38." Was all Bob had to say in response as he made his way to the door. "I just wanted to stop by and make sure you were all doing alright." He now stood in front of Dexter with his hand outstretched. Dexter obliged. Before walking out the door of the hospital room, Bob Anderson turned around to give Sensei Bo Brubaker one last dismissive glance before facing Teddy and Pat. "I never thought I would be saying this. But, you three stood foursquare when it really mattered. Most people wouldn't. I respect you for that." And Bob turned and walked away.

After a moment of silence, Teddy burst out laughing and Pat said, "I bet it damn near killed him to say that." They all laughed in agreement.

Dexter helped himself into a chair to relieve the pain in his back. He sat there, listening to the other three talk martial arts. He didn't think too much of Sensei Bo. But, the boys liked him. He was going to give them lessons now for free, forgetting about the earlier deal that they clean his dojo in exchange for the lessons. He figured having two crime-fighters like Pat and Teddy taking lessons for him would be good publicity.

Just before lunch, Gina walked into the room and handed Teddy and Pat a stack of karate magazines. "I thought you two would like these. Anything you need?"

Both thanked her profusely and neither could think of anything else they needed offhand. Gina turned to Dexter. "Come have lunch with me and my cousin, Michelle."

"Whose Michelle?" Dexter asked.

"She's my cousin. She's your age, she's single. And you are having lunch with us today."

"Is she pretty?"

"I said she's my cousin, didn't I?"

It did not occur to Dexter that he could argue with Gina. Frankly, he didn't want to. So, he got up to leave. He looked at Teddy. "Thanks for saving my life. No one's ever taken a bullet for me before."

"I'm glad I did it. I just wish we could have saved Don."

"I know."

****

Three months later, Wilbur Pedersen took his seat on the County Court bench. His first act as County Judge was to swear Tom McWilliams in as County Attorney. Mildred Pedersen had no problems at all adjusting to being a judge's mother.

There had not been enough evidence to charge Linda Birch or her daughter criminally with any of the murders, what Don told Dexter was ruled hearsay, and not a dying declaration. There was enough evidence to prevent either of them from benefitting from their husbands' deaths. Neither would collect life insurance or any other benefits. They sold off all their properties cheaply, quietly, and quickly and left town. Bob Schmidt bought up most of the property. But, Gina had some money squirreled away and bought two of the duplexes. She payed Bob a

188

commission to manage them for her. They both paid Pat and Teddy to mow and help Bob with routine maintenance.

Dexter was trying to settle into his new life as a respected lawyer. His practice grew, with Gina's help. He had lunch regularly with Gina's cousin, Michelle. He made it a point to go out drinking one Friday night a month with Pat and Teddy.

Things had turned in a big way for Dexter Smith. He started realizing more and more that Tom McWilliams was right, no lawyer knows everything. They figure it out as they go along. Dexter was figuring it out. Still, his biggest case, the Don Birch case, never even went to trial. And that bothered Dexter. He still got that feeling once in a while. The feeling that all he would ever be is some backwards hick lawyer who doesn't know shit from apple butter.

COREY BURNS is a middle aged public defender in Central Nebraska. He lives with his wife, Jeannie, and their three young daughters in Cozad, Nebraska. He has been a newspaper reporter, prison guard (for three weeks), a construction worker, farm laborer, factory worker and many other things that he either can't remember or don't warrant listing. He received his B.A. in English from Arkansas State University in 1999, at the age of 29, and his J.D. from the University of Nebraska College of Law in 2002. This is his first attempt at publishing fiction.

Special Thanks

I would like to thank Jedidiah Ayres, Benjamin Whitmer, and Max Booth III for always patiently and kindly answering questions about writing, even though we are only acquainted through social media. Thanks a lot to Andy Stock and Shawn Farritor for giving good advice to me throughout the process and reading the MS and giving great feedback and suggestions. Thanks to J. David Osborne of Broken River Books for his editing and formatting services as well as positive feedback and always being a great guy to just talk to. I especially want to thank my wife, Jeannie, for her support and encouragement throughout the years spent writing this. And thanks to my daughters for always asking how my story is going and letting me work on it when we could have been doing something together.

Made in the USA
Las Vegas, NV
27 December 2021

39568213R00113